Inkling

Kenneth Oppel

WITH ILLUSTRATIONS BY
SYDNEY SMITH

A YEARLING BOOK

This is a work of fiction. Names, characters, places, and incidents
either are the product of the author's imagination or are used
fictitiously. Any resemblance to actual persons, living or dead,
events, or locales is entirely coincidental.

Text copyright © 2018 by Firewing Productions, Inc.
Cover art and interior illustrations copyright © 2018 by Sydney Smith

All rights reserved. Published in the United States by Yearling,
an imprint of Random House Children's Books, a division of
Penguin Random House LLC, New York. Originally published in
hardcover in the United States by Knopf Books for Young Readers,
an imprint of Random House Children's Books, a division of
Penguin Random House LLC, New York, in 2018.

Yearling and the jumping horse design are registered trademarks
of Penguin Random House LLC.

Visit us on the Web! rhcbooks.com

Educators and librarians, for a variety of teaching tools,
visit us at RHTeachersLibrarians.com

Library of Congress Cataloging-in-Publication Data
is available upon request.

ISBN 978-1-5247-7284-0 (paperback)

Printed in the United States of America
10 9 8 7
First Yearling Edition 2020

FOR JULIA

CHAPTER 1

No one was awake to see it happen, except Rickman.

He was taking one of his midnight prowls, padding past the bedrooms of sleeping people, hoping to find something interesting to eat. He was nearly always hungry. Against the wall he found a dead fly, a chocolate chip, and a small piece of red crayon, which he also ate. He was not a picky cat. At the end of the hallway, he slipped into Mr. Rylance's studio. In front of the drafting table was a chair he liked, and Rickman heaved himself up. It took two tries because he was heftier than he should have been.

On the drafting table, Mr. Rylance's big sketchbook lay open. Animals and buildings and people jostled on the pages. Some pictures had scribbles through them, some were very sketchy, and others looked like they were ready to make an appearance in one of Mr. Rylance's finished graphic novels. But these were all just ideas. They had no stories to go with them yet.

When it happened, it made no noise, but Rickman saw the whole thing.

The black ink looked suddenly wet, like the pictures had been drawn that very second. The lines glistened, then trembled. From every corner of the sketchbook, the ink beaded and started slithering across the pages toward the crease in the middle. As the ink moved, it left no smear behind it, just blank page. The lines of ink joined other lines, melding into weird shapes, sometimes smooth, sometimes pointy, getting larger. When they all met in the center of the book, they formed a big black splotch, about the size of a fist. For a moment it was motionless, as if resting.

Normally, Rickman took no interest in the arts, but this was different. He put his paws on the edge of the drafting table and leaned forward for a better view.

The ink rippled, like dark water with something swimming beneath the surface. Then it was on the move again, flowing down the crease until it reached the bottom of the page. It thickened along the edge, as though it was trying to pour itself over—but it couldn't. It seemed to be stuck.

Rickman's ears flattened against his skull. A thin tendril of ink lifted from the page, maybe half an inch or so, like a tiny arm desperate to escape quicksand. Then it got slurped back in.

Next a thicker spike of ink rose up, straining, reaching over the edge of the sketchbook, one second, two, before it collapsed back. Almost a minute passed and nothing happened.

Rickman yawned, showing his still-sharp teeth. This was getting boring.

All at once the ink rippled, as if a stiff wind blew across it, and then the entire splotch contracted and rose into a little mountain peak. It trembled, tensed, and then sprang. All the ink lifted right off the sketchbook—leaving the pages totally blank—and landed with a small splash on the drafting table.

Rickman purred low and deep in his throat. This was getting interesting again. This might be something worth eating.

Already little strands of the ink splotch were being pulled back toward the sketchbook, as if it were a magnet or a black hole. The splotch struggled, fighting its way inch by inch across the drafting table. The book had a powerful pull, dragging some stringy tendrils of ink toward it. But just when they were about to touch paper, they recoiled as if burned, rejoining the main inky splotch.

When it finally reached the far edge of the drafting table—leaving no trace of ink in its wake—it came to a rest, quivering slightly like something exhausted, but also amazed, and maybe even excited, because it started doing some kind of dance. It swirled round and round, spinning itself into all kinds of strange and beautiful shapes. Like it was celebrating its freedom.

Rickman's paw came slamming down on it, claws extended. The splotch went spiky in surprise, then streaked between the cat's claws and right over the edge of the table. It scurried along the underside, tested a table leg with a black, inky tongue, and then slid itself down to the floor.

While Rickman sniffed at the drafting table, the ink started flowing across the floor. It had no plan except to get as far away as possible. When it was halfway to the door, Rickman turned and his sharp eyes caught it. But by the time he'd eased himself off the chair, the ink had seeped out into the hallway.

There was light in the hallway, so the ink made itself skinny and slunk cautiously along the baseboard. Anyone looking would have missed it, or thought it was just shadow.

But Rickman knew better. He was old, arthritic, and overweight, but he hadn't forgotten how to hunt. He prowled down the hall, head dipped low, then pounced. The ink must have sensed him coming, because it shot straight up the wall, faster than any shadow. Rickman banged his nose against the baseboard and landed clumsily on the floor. His nose wasn't the only thing that hurt. Nothing is more important to a cat than its dignity, and he glared up at the ink splotch. The fur on his back lifted. With a hiss, he leapt, claws extended.

The splotch darted higher, just out of reach, and then swelled itself into a terrifying imitation of Rickman: an enormous black cat, back humped and jagged. Its vast, inky claws shot down the wall to swat Rickman. Yowling, Rickman somersaulted backward, then bolted.

The ink shrank back into a small blob and jiggled a bit as if laughing. It left no marks on the wall as it moved higher, onto the framed poster of Mr. Rylance's best-known character, a mutant superhero called Kren.

But the moment the splotch tried to climb the glass, it slid right back down to the frame. It shuffled along a bit and tried again, with the same result, pouring off the glass like water. There was no getting a grip on this stuff! The ink gave up, moved back onto the wall, and kept going.

It wanted to find somewhere safe. When it reached a doorway, it slid inside the darkened room and down to the floor, where it paused. It sensed all the things in the room without knowing what they were. It had no words yet, no names for things like a desk, a bed, and a boy sleeping on the bed in a knotted tangle of sheets that made it look like he'd been battling something. The boy's feet were on the pillow, and his head was where his feet should have been.

Beside the bed was a pile of books, and the ink splotch stopped warily. It waited. It sent out a tiny tendril, but these books didn't try to suck it in. Only Mr. Rylance's sketchbook seemed to want to do that. The ink slid closer.

It moved over an open math textbook and erased every word, number, and diagram it touched. It actually slurped the ink into itself. The ink paused, and formed itself into an isosceles triangle, and then a rhombus, before flowing on, erasing as it went. It left a blank trail behind it like a slug trail, except it wasn't slimy. It was just shiny blank paper.

Off the math book and onto a novel. It wiped out most of the title and the cover illustration—it was in color, and the splotch seemed to like color because it gave a happy shimmer—and then found itself on a piece of illustration board.

The board had been divided up into squares and rectangles of different sizes. Most of them had stick figures penciled inside them, but in the very first squares were ink drawings. They weren't very good. There were lots of smears. The ink splotch slid across, erasing as it went, and then stopped in the middle of the board.

This seemed like a good hiding place. The splotch stretched, then made itself as small as possible. It liked it here. The feel of the creamy paper was pleasing. The ink turned itself round in circles a few times, like a dog trying to get comfortable, and then was still.

CHAPTER 2

Ethan woke up worried.

He'd stayed up late trying to draw, and that never went well. He hated drawing, but he had no choice, because his group had asked him to do the penciling and inking for their graphic novel project. Everyone, even his closest friends, assumed that since his father was a famous artist, Ethan was an amazing artist, too.

This was not true, and Ethan had known it since third grade. None of his pictures looked like what he was trying to draw. His dogs and cats and cows all looked the same; his people were weird and melty. So he'd stopped drawing altogether. When he was forced to at school, he'd just do stick figures. Everyone thought he was joking around, hiding his genius, that he could draw whatever he wanted.

So when his friends Soren, Pino, and Brady formed a

group for the graphic novel project, they'd voted for him to do the art. Soren was writing the story because he'd seen the most movies, and anyway, he already had an idea about a gorilla who lived in the zoo but was really a secret agent who beat down alien scumbags trying to take over the planet. Pino would color the finished drawings because even in kindergarten he'd never gone outside the lines, and was still very neat in general. And Brady was going to do the lettering because he was a train wreck and no one really trusted him to do anything else, and they thought it was the easiest job.

Last night, Ethan had tried to draw gorillas, getting angrier and more frustrated with each stroke of his pen. What he'd ended up with looked like a saggy marshmallow with a pig head. He'd only managed to sketch out a few panels before giving up in a rage.

And today, Ms. D was giving them a whole period to work on their projects, and everyone would see the terrible truth. He could not draw. It wasn't fair. His father could draw—but Dad wouldn't even help him, not really. Dad always said he'd help and then after dinner he'd say he was too tired, that he'd had a pen in his hand all day, and his work wasn't going well, and he didn't even want to *think* about drawing.

Ethan sighed heavily. He peeked over the side of his bed where he'd dumped his illustration board. Maybe it would look better this morning. Maybe the gorilla would look more like a gorilla.

He squinted. "What . . . ?"

It was even worse than he'd expected. He knew he'd made

some smears, but what he saw was a total mess. Parts of his drawing had been erased, and in the very middle of the spread was a huge black splotch. It looked like ink spilled from a bottle, but that didn't make any sense. He'd been using fine-tipped markers. And anyway, this ink still looked . . . wet.

He poked his finger into the middle of it. The blob went spiky as a sea urchin.

Ethan hollered.

The ink ricocheted around the illustration board, erasing more of his terrible drawings.

Ethan vaulted out of bed. The inkblot scuttled underneath it.

Ethan grabbed his hockey stick.

"There's a huge bug in my room!" he shouted.

Standing as far away as possible, he jabbed the stick under his bed.

"I think it's a tarantula!" he bellowed to the house. "If anyone cares!"

Sarah came in, in her blue-and-pink dolphin pajamas, and said:

"She wants ice cream."

"What?" Ethan said, poking under his bed some more.

Ethan's little sister was almost nine, and still talked about herself in the third person, even though everyone had been correcting her for ages. It made whatever she said sound like a story, with herself as the hero.

"Ice cream. With chocolate sauce," said Sarah, very slowly and clearly. She was holding a book with a picture of someone eating an ice cream cone.

"I'm kind of busy!" Ethan said.

Sarah had Down syndrome, and there were lots of things that were still mysteries to her, like why you couldn't just eat ice cream whenever you wanted.

A bedraggled man appeared in the doorway in his bathrobe, his hair plastered flat on one side, spiked up like a rooster's comb on the other. This was Ethan's dad, or, as Ethan called him in the mornings, Coma Dad.

He muttered, "What's, um . . . is everything . . . ?"

Ethan knew his dad hadn't had any coffee yet, because he wasn't finishing sentences.

"There's a huge bug, or tarantula, or something under my bed! It messed up my graphic novel! Probably peed all over it or something! See?"

Dad zombie-walked across the room, tilted at the waist like a hinged toy, and peered down at the messy illustration board. He glanced right and left for no apparent reason, then sat down on Ethan's bed. "Well, I'm not seeing . . . I think it's . . ."

"You hardly looked!"

Sarah walked over to Coma Dad and put her hands tenderly on either side of his face. Shaking his head gently, she gazed into his eyes and said, "Ice cream."

"Um," Coma Dad said to Ethan, his head and voice wobbling, "tarantulas, yeah, aren't even all that toxic . . . so it's not a big deal. . . ."

"With chocolate sauce," Sarah added firmly, giving her father a concerned look, like she really, really wanted him to understand this very simple idea, and why was this so difficult for him?

"Not a big deal?" exclaimed Ethan.

Coma Dad stood, took Sarah's hand, and headed for the door.

"Where are you going?" Ethan demanded.

"To the kitchen . . . to, um . . . get ice cream."

"Thanks, everyone!" Ethan shouted at his empty room.

"Thanks for helping!"

Ethan gave underneath his bed one last jab. Whatever it was, it was gone. Maybe he'd squashed it. Or maybe not. No way was he going to sleep in that bed before checking. When he got home from school, he'd drag the bed away from the wall and pull all his junk out so he could be sure it wasn't hiding, waiting for him.

He looked down at the illustration board and felt saggy. He couldn't show this to his friends. It looked even more terrible now. Everyone would know. He'd leave it at home and say he'd forgotten it.

• • •

The walk to school was only three blocks, and when he was alone, Ethan could do it in six minutes. But with Sarah it took fifteen or sometimes twenty because there were babies to admire, dogs to pat, and squirrels to holler at. Also, Sarah didn't like school, so she walked as slowly as possible. Holding her soft, starfish-shaped hand, Ethan felt her leaning backward. He was practically dragging her.

"Sarah, can you walk a little faster?" he asked.

"Of course," she said agreeably, and her steps, if anything, became tinier.

"We're going to be late!"

"You naughty squirrel!" she bellowed at an innocent rodent that was just trying to scrounge a meal.

Finally they reached the schoolyard, and Ethan steered Sarah carefully around kids throwing tennis balls, kids shooting hoops, kids doing yo-yos. His friend Pino was playing monkey in the middle near the gym, and Ethan wanted to get over there. He spotted Sarah's educational assistant, Mrs. Hunter, and led Sarah toward her, pulling pretty hard. Then he felt mean because Sarah insisted on kissing him good-bye twice, and hugging him. She locked her arms around his neck so tightly he had to gently pry her loose.

"I'll just be upstairs from you!" he told her, like he did every day.

"Have a good day, sweetie," Sarah told him. "Be safe!" And Ethan felt a hard squeeze in his throat because this was what Mom used to say to them.

When he turned to go join the game, his best friend, Soren, was standing right behind him, looking startled. Soren always looked startled. He hadn't blinked since fourth grade. His older brother, Barnaby, had let him read too many scary comics and watch too many horror movies, and now it was like Soren was afraid to blink in case something crept up on him.

"How's the drawing coming?" Soren asked.

"Great! It's going great!" When you were lying, it was important to repeat yourself and add exclamation marks. "Except some weird bug peed on it. Messed it up a little. But I'll fix it."

"Do bugs pee?" Soren asked.

"Sure! Sure they do!"

"Maybe it was Squeaker," said Soren without blinking.

Squeaker was the hamster Ethan had when he was ten. Squeaker lasted exactly four days before Dad left the cage open and the hamster escaped somewhere into the house. Squeaker was never seen again, but Ethan sometimes wondered if it had survived in the basement and was getting huge and strange.

"It wasn't Squeaker," Ethan said. "I saw it."

"Weird. So can I see the drawings?"

Ethan winced. "I forgot them."

Soren's eyes widened even more. "But we're getting first period to work on it! The inking is due end of next week, you know."

"Plenty of time!" said Ethan. "Don't worry!"

He always felt like he had to reassure Soren so he didn't have a heart attack or something.

"Well, I guess we could work on the story some more," Soren suggested.

"Great idea," said Ethan as the bell rang.

• • •

After announcements, everyone arranged themselves into their groups. Some people were inking; others were already coloring and starting on the lettering. Ethan felt bad about letting down his group, but mostly he was just relieved he wouldn't have to do any drawing in front of them.

"I didn't think bugs peed," Pino remarked after Ethan explained why he didn't have the artwork.

"I think it was the hamster," said Soren.

"My cousin had a hamster that escaped and ate all their suitcases," said Brady.

"Why don't we work on the story," Ethan said.

"Yeah. I think the ending's weak," Soren said.

"I thought it was good," said Brady.

Brady liked everything. Ethan had known him since first grade, and there wasn't a movie or book he hadn't liked. There was no food he didn't like either. You could give him all the scraped-up bits from the bottom of the fridge and he'd like it. Once he'd chewed gum he found on the ground.

"What do you think, Pino?" Ethan asked.

Everyone waited. Pino was one of those kids who knew the best way to do everything. The best way to arm-wrestle. The best yo-yo tricks. The best way to make an origami swan. Ethan wished he had a big brother who would teach him all this stuff. Dad always managed to be busy.

"I like it, too," said Pino, "but maybe we could make it even cooler. . . ."

Ethan tuned out as his friends talked about the gorilla and whether he needed to save the *entire* universe, or whether just the planet was enough. He looked over at the next table, where Vika's group was working.

He stood up a little in his seat so he could catch a glimpse of her artwork. She'd finished inking an entire two-page spread, and it was amazing.

She caught him looking. "Don't even think of copying me."

"Why would I copy *that*?" Ethan said, wrinkling his nose.

Vika's eyes narrowed. "Well, you'd better copy something, because it doesn't look like you have anything."

"I forgot it at home!"

"Uh-huh. I hear a hamster peed on it." She smirked.

"Maybe you peed on it because it was so bad."

Ethan glared. Vika Worthington was, without question, the best artist in their grade. Last year she'd made fun of his stick figures and said he couldn't draw to save his life. To get her back, Ethan told her that her drawings sucked and that his father, who just happened to be a world-famous artist, thought so, too. He finished up by telling her that she could kiss good-bye her dreams of being a famous artist, or even a lousy artist. Vika was taller than him, and she'd been doing martial arts for years, so she tornado-kicked him into a garbage can. The can tipped over and Ethan sort of fell into it. It was after lunch and it was full of everyone's banana peels and empty yogurt containers and things with ketchup on them. That was over a year ago, but he had not forgotten.

Ethan had read a lot of comics, and Vika might not quite be a supervillain, but she was definitely an archenemy.

What made it even weirder and more complicated was that her father was Dad's publisher. Karl Worthington was the founder and owner of Prometheus Comix. When he'd started his company, it only had a couple of artists, and one of them was Ethan's dad. But since then, after publishing Dad's entire Kren series, Prometheus had gotten a lot bigger. Sometimes, at comic conventions or book signings or parties, Ethan ended up in the same room or at the same table as Vika, and they ignored each other. Amazingly, their fathers didn't have a clue that their kids were mortal enemies.

"Our graphic novel is going to kill yours," Ethan told her now.

"Maybe if your dad does it for you. But it doesn't seem like your dad's doing much of anything lately."

Ethan saw an angry flash of red-and-black lightning inside his head. "Shut up, Vika!"

"Sixth graders!" said Ms. D, looking up from her desk. "I know you are being hardworking and respectful of your fellow classmates. Let's stay focused on our work, please."

CHAPTER 3

While Ethan was at school, back home the ink splotch was exploring.

From the top of the doorway, it peeped into Peter Rylance's studio. Pen in hand, Ethan's dad hunched over the big sketchbook on his drafting table. The sight of that sketchbook sent a shudder through the ink splotch. It remembered pulling free, and how the thirsty pages had tried to pull it back.

The book seemed to frighten Mr. Rylance, too, because he kept leaning back and shaking his head and making loud grunts. Once he even pounded the book with his fist. He hadn't yet drawn a single thing on the blank pages.

Cautiously, the ink slid down the hallway, high up the wall, keeping watch for the cat. Inside Sarah's bedroom, it flowed over to a shelf of books near her bed. The ink liked

books—normal books, not that terrible sketchbook. The ink seeped over one of the covers, erasing part of a colorful pig, and then slipped inside the pages. It was an alphabet book, and the ink moved across As and Ds and Js, absorbing them, and practicing making the shapes on its own as it slid around, erasing words and pictures. It left the book completely blank.

Next there was a sticker book filled with happy faces and sad faces and all sorts of emojis. The ink slurped these up, too. Then came a book about babies. It was one of Sarah's favorites. The ink splotch seemed to like it as well. It poured itself over pictures of kittens and puppies, a baby kangaroo peeping from a pouch, human babies being cuddled by their mothers. The last picture was of a mama gorilla with a baby gorilla holding on to her back. The ink absorbed that one, too.

With all this new ink, the splotch felt very energetic and swiftly finished off a few short chapter books, practicing all its new letters and words on the now-blank pages. It was learning a lot. By this time, the splotch had swelled up and was rolling itself lazily across the floor. It lurched out into the hallway, sticking close to the wall (it hadn't forgotten the cat), and returned to Ethan's room.

After a brief rest, it explored the insides of Ethan's chest of drawers—socks, underwear, T-shirts, nothing very interesting. The top of the chest of drawers, however, *was* very interesting. It was cluttered with all kinds of strange things: playing cards, and colorful multi-sided dice, and a shark tooth, and a model of a volcano with lava hardened on the sides. Propped against the wall was a bulletin board. On it was tacked a picture of Ethan and his mother, both smiling.

The ink flowed onto the photograph, slowly lapping over Ethan and his mother, erasing them both.

The ink paused. This was important. It didn't know why,

only that it was. There was something the ink was supposed to do, something it was supposed to find. What was it?

The ink seeped away, pausing, as if looking back at the photograph it had erased. Then it flowed to the floor and over to the illustration board where it had rested last night.

Next to the illustration board was a crinkled piece of paper covered with words. It was actually the first page of the story Soren had written for the graphic novel. This was the script that Ethan was supposed to follow when doing the drawings. The ink moved across the text. It didn't just take the ink inside; it took the story, too.

The ink pulled itself onto the edge of the illustration board. For a moment, it was still. Then it nudged forward and erased Ethan's work, all of it, smears included. All it left was the borders of the panels and Ethan's penciled stick figures.

It rested thoughtfully another moment, and then, with a tiny black tendril of ink, it began to draw.

• • •

Last period was math, and Ms. D told them to get out their textbooks so they could review their homework. Mind elsewhere, Ethan started paging through his text.

He knew he was in deep trouble with the graphic novel project. He needed help. The few times Dad had actually given Ethan a lesson, Ethan worried that his father was getting impatient, and worried even more that his father was disappointed in him. He'd say things like "You'll get better with practice" or "You can't really teach art." Ethan hoped this wasn't true, because he needed to get a lot better, and fast. He needed his father to teach him to draw *tonight*.

When Ethan got to the right place in his math textbook, he stared in confusion. It looked like someone had painted a thick, wavy white line across both pages. But it wasn't paint. It was nothing. Part of the book had just been erased. It hadn't been like this last night. . . .

That weird bug thing! It had done this!

"Ethan, would you start us off with question twelve?"

Ethan looked frantically at the textbook. Question twelve was gone. His eyes flicked to his exercise book, where his answers were written. You were supposed to show your work, but Ethan hardly ever did.

"I got eighteen," he said.

"Good. Now, can you tell us how?"

"Yeaaaaaah," he said, and then guessed. "I took . . . both sides of the triangle and squared them, and then . . . yeah."

"This isn't a question about triangles, Ethan." She started walking toward him. "Did you actually do your homework?"

He panicked and slammed the textbook shut, then tried to make things better by giving a big stretch and yawn. He lifted his exercise book so Ms. D could see his answers. She glanced at it but then opened up his textbook. She stared at the erased pages.

"This is school property, Ethan. Other students are going to need this book next year."

"I don't know how that happened!"

"See me after school, please. You'll need to fill in all the missing words and numbers. Very neatly."

"Oh, man," said Ethan.

Down the aisle, Vika smirked at him.

After class, Soren came up to him, his forehead creased with concern. "You're going to work on the graphic novel tonight, right?"

"Yeah, as soon as I finish detention," he said.

Soren looked around and then overhead, as if something might be hanging there, ready to drop. "Everyone else is a lot further ahead."

"Hey, it'll be fine!!" said Ethan, adding two exclamation marks.

His plan was to go home and ask his dad for help—a kind of crash course in drawing gorillas and, well, drawing in general.

"Hey, Ethan?"

He looked over to see Heather Lee walking toward him shyly. Maybe something good was actually going to happen today.

"Oh, hey," he said, feeling the heat in his cheeks. "Hi, Heather."

From her bag, she pulled an envelope. "I was just wondering if—"

A party! She was going to invite him to her birthday party or something!

"—you could give this to your father."

Ethan's hopeful smile disintegrated, and he plastered a fake one on top. "Yeah, sure, totally, I'll give it to him."

Heather beamed. "Really? Thanks so much. I love your dad's Kren series so much! I've wanted to write him a fan letter for ages!"

• • •

It took Ethan almost an hour to fill in all the erased bits in his math textbook. Ms. D was very particular. She made him use correction fluid when he made a mistake or was too messy. He'd never liked geometry, but now he never wanted to see another polygon or parallelogram as long as he lived.

Walking home, he planned out how to get help from Dad. Even though he started his days as Coma Dad, chances were that by the end of the day he'd have morphed into Grumpy Dad. He absolutely didn't like being disturbed during his work hours, so Ethan decided to wait until five-thirty, after Dad had picked up Sarah from her after-school program, after he had a glass of wine in his hand. That was the plan.

When he got home, he'd barely kicked off his shoes when he heard his father call out, "Ethan?"

Surprised, Ethan walked down the hallway. His father was standing in the doorway of his studio, holding his sketchbook.

As long as Ethan could remember, Dad had a sketchbook on the go. The covers changed, the size changed, but the inside was always a magical world. He loved paging through them, just looking at the things his father drew from quick observation, or conjured from his imagination. It was like his dad was sightseeing in some new world, jotting down all the strange, wonderful things he saw. Ethan would have given anything to be able to do that—with only a few lines, to create a person you could tell was sad, just by his shoulders. It all seemed to come so easily to his father.

"Were you in my studio this morning? Or last night?"

Ethan frowned. "No."

Dad opened up his sketchbook. "There's two pages missing."

"What?" He went closer.

"You didn't cut them out?"

"No!"

It wasn't a completely unfair question. Ethan had actually done it, just once—razored out a couple of pages to show his friends at school what his dad was working on. To prove that his dad really was Peter Rylance, and to make himself more popular. Still, that had been a long time ago.

"If I had, you'd see lines where I cut," Ethan said. "There's no lines!"

His father bent the book back and peered into the crease. "Then why're they gone, Ethan? Drawings don't just disappear!"

"I don't know!"

His father sighed. "They were good. I was really close to something."

Ethan heard this phrase a lot. His father got really close, but never close enough to actually *start* a new graphic novel.

His sketchbooks were full of sketches, but he hadn't finished anything in two years. And that was why, in the afternoons, Dad became Grumpy Dad.

There was everyday grumpy, when he'd talk in grunts and sigh a lot. Then there was medium grumpy, when he'd rub the space between his eyes really hard, and snap at Ethan for messing up the fridge. Then there was super grumpy, when he'd yell at Sarah for watching the TV too loud, and say his career was over and no one liked good things anymore, so what was the point of even trying.

Ethan knew this was probably going to be a super grumpy day. His hopes of getting drawing help crumbled. No way could he ask Dad now. But . . . there was one thing that might cheer him up.

"Oh, here," said Ethan.

He dug Heather Lee's fan letter out of his pocket and handed it to his dad.

His father winged it into the recycling bin inside his studio.

"You didn't even read it!" Ethan cried.

"I know exactly what it says."

"You can't!"

"Believe me, I do. I've had thousands of them."

Ethan knew his father got lots of fan letters—not as many as he used to, but still a good number. He'd never thought much about what his dad did with them, but throwing them out unread seemed so mean. Ethan went to the recycling bin and fished out the letter.

His dad gave a weary sigh. "Fine. Open it."

Ethan carefully tore the side of the envelope and pulled out the letter.

"Okay," said his dad. "Here we go. It'll say how he or she—"

"She."

"—loves my Kren series, maybe even more than any other books she's ever read. The third book was probably her favorite in the series. Then she'll tell me how upset she was when Kren died."

Reading hastily, Ethan had to admit his father was right so far.

"She'll ask, or maybe even beg, me to write another book in the series, and bring Kren back to life. She might even say I'm a terrible person for killing Kren, or call me a rude name."

"There's nothing rude in here," Ethan said. Heather wasn't like that.

"And she might suggest a story line so I can bring Kren back to life and continue the series."

Ethan folded up the letter. "Okay, she did give you an idea."

"Maybe a lightning bolt, or a magical elixir . . ."

"Okay, yes, but still . . ."

Not for the first time, Ethan wondered what it would be like to get letters, even just one, telling him he was an amazing artist or storyteller, or an amazing anything.

"Doesn't it make you feel good at all?" Ethan asked.

Dad grunted.

"You get letters every day from kids who love your series!"

What Ethan loved most about Kren was that he seemed like the best friend you could ever have. Yes, he was a weird-looking mutant created by evil scientists, and sure, he lost his temper sometimes and threw cars around or made volcanoes erupt, but in his spare time he went to school, helped out at an animal shelter, and made these incredible banana splits with more toppings than you could imagine.

"Yeah, well," Dad said, "I finished that series a long time ago."

Kren had made him famous, but now he was blocked. That was the word Dad used. The way he said it, it wasn't just a little chunk of concrete in the road—it was a huge black stone wall topped with barbed wire and guard towers.

He said he just didn't have any ideas that got him excited. His publisher wanted him to do more Kren books. Kids wanted him to do more. But he wouldn't. So every day he sat at his drafting table and sketched, and at the end of almost every day he was grumpy.

"Have you ever thought of doing it?" Ethan asked. "Bringing him back?"

"Kren?"

"Why not?"

His father said nothing for a moment, then rubbed hard between his eyes. "Sometimes people die. That's just the way it is."

CHAPTER 4

In his bedroom, Ethan dumped his backpack and dropped heavily into his chair. He flipped open the laptop. He had a ton of work to do—and he knew he also needed to check under his bed for tarantulas or worse—but he couldn't face any of it yet. If he could just play a game or two of *Realm of Evil,* he'd feel better.

His screen lit up. He logged on and started fighting orcs. His dad could be such a jerk. Accusing him of stealing his stupid sketches.

Why didn't he just do another Kren book? Everyone wanted one, and at least he'd be doing something useful instead of grumping at everyone all the time.

From the corner of his eye, he could see his graphic novel project on the floor, but he refused to turn and face it head-on. It was too depressing. He cut off more orc heads, but there was something about the project that kept nagging at his eye. He turned and looked—

And kept looking. Because even though the project was exactly where he'd left it, it couldn't have been more different. Ethan jumped from his chair and crouched in front of it.

Panel after panel, the entire first page was drawn and inked. Every scene he'd sketched with stick figures was finished. And it was so good! The zoo, the animals, the secret passages—and the gorilla! The gorilla was just the way he'd imagined but been completely unable to draw.

Ethan hunched over it and felt a flood of relief, and also happiness. Not just because the work was so good, but because he thought his father had done it for him. Dad must have come into his room while he was at school, and felt sorry for him, and done the first page, just to help him out, and show him the way!

Something edged out from under his bed.

Ethan didn't holler this time, but he dropped the illustration board and scuttled back on his bum. The inky blotch seeped onto the blank half of the board and stopped.

If anything, it was bigger than it had been this morning, but it definitely wasn't a bug. There were no squiggly legs or antennae. And it was completely flat. He would've said it was ink, except that it left no stain behind it. And ink didn't move on its own.

Ethan patted behind him for his hockey stick. Whatever

this thing was, he was going to hammer it to smithereens. He kept his eyes on it—and had the strangest feeling it was keeping its eyes on him, too. Which was impossible, since it had no eyes. Still, it was giving an excellent impression of being watchful, and somehow expectant.

"What are you?" Ethan murmured to himself.

The splotch started to move, and Ethan's hand found the hockey stick and gripped tight. Staying on the board, the ink splotch swirled itself into a perfect question mark.

Ethan stared. "What's that mean? Are you asking me a question, or answering one?"

The question mark pulsed faintly on the board.

"You don't know what you are?" Ethan said. "Is that what you mean?"

Ethan gasped as the ink swirled with startling speed into a big smiley face.

"Okay," said Ethan. "You're smiling at me now. Does that mean yes? You don't know what you are?"

The ink morphed itself into a thumbs-up sign.

Ethan couldn't help grinning. Whatever this thing was, it seemed quite cheerful. It didn't seem like it wanted to eat him or anything. His grip on the hockey stick loosened but didn't release.

"If you don't know what you are, do you know where you're from?"

He jerked back with a start as the ink exploded all across the blank half of the illustration board. Then, with amazing speed, all the splatter marks formed themselves into little sketches: plants and people and buildings.

"Hey," Ethan said, frowning, "that looks like Dad's stuff."

One of the drawings turned into a bouncing thumbs-up sign.

"Okay, so Dad made some drawings, and . . ."

Suddenly the drawings all flowed together into a big splotch. The splotch roiled and gave a mighty jerk, as if trying to pull itself right off the paper.

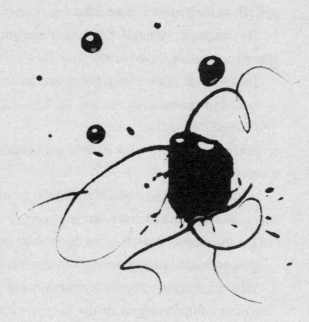

Ethan shook his head, wondering what on earth it was doing. After a second pull, the inky blotch sprang off the illustration board like a Slinky toy and landed on the floor, a little closer to Ethan.

He shuffled back, watching intently. The ink quivered for

a second and then formed itself into a cat with sharp claws.

"Hey, is that Rickman?" Ethan asked.

The cat picture dissolved back into a blob and scurried frantically across the floor.

Ethan stood up, gripping the hockey stick, worried this thing had gone crazy. What if it jumped onto him next? But it was darting fearfully this way and that, like it was trying to escape something.

"I don't understand," said Ethan.

The ink stopped and crept stealthily back toward the illustration board. It slid onto it, and then very intentionally pushed a black tendril over one of the beautiful drawings, erasing it completely.

"Hey!" said Ethan. "Be careful!"

The ink pulled back and with a delicate paintbrush-shaped tendril redrew the work it had erased, exactly.

Ethan exhaled. His own thoughts felt like tiny balls of black ink ricocheting around his head.

The ink splotch moved to the blank half of the illustration board and waited expectantly.

"You're telling me a story," Ethan said.

He got a thumbs-up for that.

"So. The pictures in my dad's sketchbook all kind of ran together and . . . you're the ink?"

He got a happy face.

"And then you jumped off the sketchbook?"

That would explain the blank pages Dad had complained

about. No one had taken the pages—the ink had literally run away!

"But it was hard work," Ethan continued as the ink quivered. "To get off. And then you got chased—was that Rickman?"

The ink formed itself into a question mark again.

"Rickman. A cat! Our cat!"

He got a happy face, which quickly turned into a sad face. Ethan couldn't help smiling: the idea of Rickman as a terrifying animal was pretty funny. Rickman could hardly hop up onto the sofa.

Ethan moved a little closer to the illustration board. "So you ran away from Rickman and ended up in my room?"

The smiley face bobbed up and down.

"And you got onto my drawings and . . ." He remembered his math textbook. "You erase whatever you touch! That was you! I got in trouble!"

The smiley face drooped.

"It's okay," said Ethan. "And you did all this?" He pointed at the drawings for his graphic novel.

The sad face lifted into a happy one and nodded.

"You drew all this today? It's amazing!"

Ethan sat back with a sigh, trying to make sense of it all. The ink of his father's sketches had somehow come to life. And this ink had the power to erase—and draw! And what pictures it could do! He gazed at the finished art again.

"But how did you know the story?"

He hadn't noticed the crumpled page of Soren's script

until now, probably because it was completely blank, except for a few stray letters at the edges.

"You read his story?" Ethan breathed.

What other explanation could there be? It was one thing to draw a gorilla, but these pictures were clearly based on his stick figures and the scenes in the story.

"You can read?"

As Ethan watched in amazement, a tiny point of ink stretched out and shakily wrote:

A BIT

For a moment Ethan couldn't say anything. Then he asked, "How?"

The first words slurped back into the ink and were replaced by:

BOOKS

"This is incredible," Ethan said. This creature had taught itself to read, and write, all in the space of a day! He shuffled closer to the paper. He was still a little nervous being near the ink—it could move so quickly—but he was pretty sure it wasn't dangerous. And it was certainly smart.

"Do you have a name?"

NO

Ethan thought for a moment. Everything needed a name. What did you call a thing made of ink? An ink thing? Inkthing. Inkling!

"Inkling!" he said. "Do you like that name?"

The ink was still for a moment, as if considering. A tiny tip reached out and wrote:

YES

And then Inkling wrote his name on the board, not just once, but several times in different types of letters, plain letters and fancy letters, faster and faster. When Inkling was done writing his name, the ink flowed back together and formed a happy face.

Ethan smiled, too. "So, you can see me?"

YES

He wondered how it was possible, since Inkling didn't seem to have any eyes. Then again, Inkling didn't seem to have any ears either, and he could hear.

Inkling started to draw. In awe Ethan watched as the lines appeared on the paper, sometimes fine, sometimes thick. Head, face, eyes, nose, mouth, hair, shading, texture. Inkling never once erased a line or made a smear. And in under a minute, Inkling had drawn an amazing picture of him. Except . . .

Ethan tilted his head. In the picture, he was younger by several years. With a start, he recognized himself from the laser-printed photograph of him and Mom. He stood and looked at his bulletin board. The picture was just a white rectangle.

"Hey!" he said, turning back to Inkling. "What did you do?"

It was hard to talk because of the lump in his throat.

Inkling formed himself into a question mark.

"The photograph of me and my mom!" he said, fighting to keep his voice low, even though he was suddenly angry. "You erased it!"

ERASD?

"Yeah, you . . . you moved across it, and now it's gone!"

I NEED INK

"Well, put her back! You need to bring her back!"

Inkling slid off the paper and across the floor. He flowed up to the top of the chest of drawers and onto the bulletin board. At the edge of the blank photograph, Inkling paused and then began to draw. Even though Inkling himself was all blackness, he seemed to contain every color. Line by line, Ethan's mother reappeared, like some miracle. Ethan's eyes prickled. Her image was just as vivid as before—if anything, more vivid, because the original photo had faded in the sunlight, but this one looked like it had been taken yesterday.

"Thanks," said Ethan, clearing his throat. "There's some things you shouldn't erase, okay?"

Silently, on the wooden surface of his chest of drawers, Inkling wrote:

WHR IS MOM?

Ethan hadn't needed to answer this question in a while, and he was startled by how much it hurt, just to think the words.

"She died."

DIED?

"Gone. Forever."

Inkling was still, as if he couldn't think of anything to say. Ethan went and sat down on the edge of his bed, staring at the artwork. Inkling slid onto the illustration board and pointed at the drawings.

GOOD?

"Yeah. I couldn't draw like this in a hundred years."

Inkling immediately started drawing the next panel. Ethan watched, hypnotized. It was a lot like his father's style, but not quite. He chewed at the inside of his mouth.

"Stop," he said.

Inkling stopped.

NO GOOD?

"No, it's fantastic. It's just . . ."

How could he do any of the art himself now? Whatever he did next would be so bad it would be obvious someone else had done the first part. He'd have to scrap the whole thing and start over.

But how could he get rid of Inkling's art? It was so good.

And he owed it to his group to give them decent art, didn't he? They'd asked him, and he'd said yes, and they were counting on him. Soren had already worked hard on the story, and Pino would be a perfectionist with the color, and Brady—well, Brady might mess up the lettering. But still, it wasn't fair if they all got a bad grade because of his terrible drawings.

Why not let Inkling finish the art? It wasn't like Ethan would be doing nothing. He'd still sketch in the panels with his stick figures, and then all Inkling would have to do was turn them into drawings.

"Maybe just a little more for now," Ethan told Inkling.

Everyone was going to be amazed tomorrow when he brought this in. He couldn't wait to see Vika's face—and Heather Lee's especially. She'd be really impressed. But if he had too much finished, they might get suspicious. "And make it just a little bit messy, please."

MESY?

"Yeah, like this." He licked his finger and smeared the art.

Enthusiastically, Inkling swiped a gorilla picture and turned it into a blob.

"Maybe not so much," Ethan said.

Inkling quickly repaired his work but left it sloppy.

"Exactly," Ethan said. "Here, I'll rough in the next few panels."

From his backpack, he pulled out the crumpled second page of Soren's story. With stick figures, Ethan filled two more panels, making sure to mark in space for the speech bubbles.

"It's this little bit here," he told Inkling, pointing to Soren's text.

Inkling flowed over the sentences, erasing them as he absorbed the ink, and then returned to the illustration board.

Spellbound, Ethan watched. Sometimes Inkling started with a fine point; other times it was more like a brushstroke. His marks could be incredibly precise, or blurry, like when Gorilla was running from the evil Trog.

Ethan paid particular attention to how he drew the gorilla, building him line by line. He remembered how he'd watch his father draw when he was younger—and it had always thrilled him, to see things come to life. Dad could draw anything: Ethan only had to yell it out, and it would appear on paper.

When Inkling finished the two panels, he stopped.

"Wow," said Ethan. "Thanks!"

He looked at Inkling and was amazed all over again. What kind of creature was he? How did he even exist?

"Um," said Ethan. "Are you hungry or anything?"

HUNGRY?

Ethan felt slightly foolish but still thought it was only polite to ask.

"Food, or water—or something to put inside you?"

INK!

Ethan laughed. "Yeah, okay . . . stay here."

STAY?

"Don't move anywhere."

OKAY

He ran to the back room and grabbed a stack of old newspapers from the recycling bin. When he was returning to his room, his father was just leaving his studio.

"What're those for?" he asked.

"School project," Ethan said.

His dad nodded. "I'm off to pick up Sarah."

He looked at his dad's face, tried to read it. Another lousy day at work.

"Okay," said Ethan. "See you soon."

He closed the door to his room behind him and found Inkling waiting obediently in exactly the same position. He put the newspaper down beside Inkling.

"There you go," he said.

Inkling eagerly slithered onto the pile. He opened a big triangular mouth, like the Pac-Man character, and skidded across the front page, sucking the ink into him. Entire paragraphs disappeared, and then entire pages. Ethan kept flipping pages, and if he didn't turn quick enough, Inkling just slid right underneath and slurped up the ink from the opposite side.

He demolished the entire front section before he started to flag. He looked bigger; in fact, he looked a bit bloated. There was a bulge in his middle, and he was dragging it around like Santa Claus's sack.

Inkling slumped, squishing out across a half-eaten page, and went so quiet Ethan could only assume he was sleeping. He looked for signs of breathing or movement but couldn't see any. He didn't want to disturb Inkling, who obviously needed rest. Gently he pushed the newspapers under his bed.

And then he heard the front door open, and his father was back from picking up Sarah, and she was hollering for him, like she always did the moment she got home.

• • •

Sarah plonked her fox toy in front of Ethan and looked at him expectantly.

"And what's wrong with Foxy?" Ethan said, a red plastic stethoscope dangling from his neck. They were sitting on the green sofa in the living room. So far he'd done checkups on four dogs, an elephant, a skunk, and something that didn't look like any creature on earth.

Sarah launched into an incredibly complicated story about all the dangerous things Foxy had done. Ethan zoned out—he'd heard most of these stories many times, and anyway, he was finding it hard to concentrate, knowing that in his bedroom, right now, was some kind of impossible creature made of intelligent ink. He felt like he'd swallowed an entire bottle of soda pop and was close to bursting.

At that moment, Rickman hauled himself onto the sofa and stepped gingerly onto Sarah's lap, purring hopefully. Rickman adored Sarah and was always rubbing against her, hoping for a pat or a warm place to curl up. Sarah, however, did not return Rickman's affection.

"Get off, Icklan!" she said, pushing him away with her pudgy hands.

"Be gentle, Sarah," Ethan told her. "He just likes you."

"She is too busy!" Sarah said, wrinkling her nose. "She is talking about Foxy."

"*I'm* talking about Foxy," Ethan corrected her. He felt sorry for Rickman and gave him a pat between his ears, but the cat just flicked his tail and walked off.

Ethan turned his attention back to Sarah, waiting impatiently to find out what was wrong with Foxy so he could treat him. He was hoping he'd get to set a broken bone, or remove a thorn, or do minor surgery, but in the end, it was the usual: a scraped knee.

Ethan cleaned Foxy's imaginary wound, put on an imaginary bandage, and then checked his heartbeat—something Sarah demanded every time, regardless of the injury.

"Strong and steady," Ethan said, standing. "Okay, I think we've done everyone."

"Just one more," said Sarah.

"I said eight and we did nine!"

"You can't forget Caspar," she said earnestly, as if only a total monster could do such a thing.

So he sat down and examined Caspar, wondering, *When's the last time Dad did this?* Dad was in the kitchen, getting dinner ready, and checking his phone while he stirred a pot.

"Frisbee!" Sarah said.

"No, Sarah, I think it's almost dinnertime anyway."

"Oh, honey, you can do it," she said, as if Ethan had low self-esteem. "Just ten throws. Deal?" She gravely extended her small hand.

Ethan exhaled and shook. "Okay."

At least he got to be outside. Frisbee with Sarah usually involved her whipping it into the cedar shrubs along the back fence. It was more like fetch, really. Sarah threw. Ethan scrounged around in the bushes, twigs scratching at his face. The Frisbee was green and said "Dinosaur Provincial Park." Every time he found the Frisbee, he thought, *Mom was still alive then.*

They'd been camping near the river, and his best memory was of the four of them sitting outside the tent, playing cards. Mom and Sarah were on the same team. He and Sarah had some kind of fizzy cranberry drink, and his parents each had a glass of wine. It was dusk, and the breeze made the leaves of the big trees rustle, and lights were twinkling from the other campsites, and all four of them were together and happy.

"Okay," Ethan said to Sarah, "three more throws."

"Is it Sarah's birthday yet?" she asked.

"Is it *my* birthday. No, three more sleeps!"

"She's having a party!"

"Yep," said Ethan. He wondered if Dad had remembered to invite everyone. "Last throw!"

Sarah threw it right to him.

"Hey, that was really good! That was your best throw yet!"

"Yes," she said, like she'd known how to do it all along, but just preferred sending him into the bushes like a rodent.

"Dinner!" Dad called from the door.

• • •

When Ethan returned to his room after the meal, Inkling was drawing on a blank piece of newsprint. Ethan caught only a few details—a corner of a bed, but not a normal bed; this one looked like it was metal, and had wheels—before Inkling quickly erased everything.

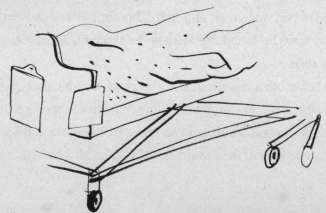

"What were you drawing?" Ethan asked.

DON'T KNOW

Ethan nodded. "Okay." He didn't feel like it was polite to pry. He looked at Inkling and wondered how a splotch of ink could seem so much like a someone instead of a something. He'd been drawing, just for himself, something private. What else did he do and think about? Something suddenly occurred to Ethan.

"Will you stay?" he asked.

NOT MOVE?

"Well, you can move, but only here, in my room." He indicated the space with his hands. "Inside the house. But don't leave."

Inkling was still. Ethan wondered if he was explaining this well enough.

"You'll stay inside and help me finish the drawings?" He mimed drawing, then patted the floor again. "For a little while. You won't go anywhere else?"

I STAY, Inkling wrote.

CHAPTER 5

When Ethan woke up the next morning, there were a few seconds before he remembered Inkling and the amazing things that had happened yesterday. Then he leapt up, reached under the bed, and gently dragged out the stack of newspaper. Inkling wasn't on top. He riffled through the pages without finding him.

"Inkling?"

He checked around his desk and on top of his chest of drawers, surprised by the panicky flutter of his heart.

"Inkling, where are you?"

Then, through the wall, he heard Sarah giggling in her bedroom.

"Do it again!" she said, as if talking to a pet.

Ethan inhaled sharply and hurried to her room. She was

in her pajamas, sitting on the floor, encircled by her favorite stuffed animals and dolls. A big picture book was open in front of her.

"And again!" she said, and brought her balled fist down hard on the book. "Splat!"

All the ink splashed across the page, and she giggled with delight, rocking back and forth. Inkling collected himself into a big ball in the middle of the page and jiggled as if chuckling.

Sarah raised her hand again. "And . . . splat!" she shouted. Inkling obligingly sprayed himself all over the page.

"Ethan, look!" Sarah said as he came closer.

"Wow," Ethan said, sitting down beside her.

This time, Sarah jabbed her hand into the middle of Inkling and started finger-painting with him across the paper. Then she lifted her hands in front of her brother's face solemnly and said, "Not dirty. Not one bit dirty!"

"That's so cool, Sarah," Ethan said.

"Splat!" said Sarah, smacking Inkling yet again.

Ethan had to admit, it looked very satisfying.

"Be a good puppy!" Sarah said, pointing her finger.

Obediently, Inkling shaped himself into a dog, his tongue lolling.

Sarah laughed. She'd been asking for a puppy for almost a year now. Dad had tried to suggest an easier pet— a fish, a hamster ("After what happened to Squeaker?" Ethan said), a newt—but she had never changed her mind. It had to be a dog, and Dad was absolutely not willing to get a dog. Ethan knew that Dad had bought her a robotic dog for her birthday. It was very lifelike. Its eyes opened and closed, and its head and mouth moved. Its tail wagged. Its sounds were realistic. Ethan wondered if the dog would be as big a hit as Inkling.

The puppy walked off the pages of the book and scampered around on the floor. Sarah had him roll over. When she put her hand on his back, he wagged his tail, then turned his head and licked her hand with his inky tongue.

"She gives licks!" Sarah exclaimed.

"It's a she?" Ethan asked her. He'd automatically assumed Inkling was a he, and his sister assumed Inkling was a she. He supposed it didn't matter one bit.

"Yes! Lucy!"

She'd already named it. Ethan looked at his little sister. Happiness beamed from her face like the ray from a lighthouse.

When Ethan heard his father's zombie footsteps approaching in the hallway, he grabbed the picture book and dropped it in front of Inkling. "Into the book!" he whispered, tapping the page. "Stay!"

Inkling scurried onto the paper just as Dad entered the room.

"It's time, um . . . to get . . . ," Dad was saying.

"She has a puppy!" Sarah said, pointing at the blob in the book.

"That doesn't . . . ," said Dad, rubbing his eyes, "look like . . ."

In a split second, Inkling re-formed himself into a puppy.

"Sarah and I were reading," Ethan told his dad.

"Uh-huh," said Dad, looking at the book, confused. "Now . . . yeah . . . clothes."

"Lucy!" Sarah shouted, picking up the book. "Give lick!"

But Inkling was on his best behavior and stayed perfectly still.

"She really wants a dog," Ethan told his dad.

"Well, maybe for her birthday," Dad replied, finishing his first sentence of the day.

• • •

When Ethan took out the illustration board to show his group during work period, they all just stared for a few seconds.

"Did I tell you?" said Soren, eyes wide. "Did I tell you this man could draw!"

"This is fantastic!" said Brady.

"Wow!" Pino said. "Ethan, I was starting to get a little worried, but this stuff's incredible. Now we can get to work coloring and lettering."

"Yeah," said Soren, "and me and Ethan can rough in the next pages."

Ms. D wandered over and nodded approvingly.

"Very nice. Now, I've got to do some photocopying," she told the class, and left the room.

Other kids came over to have a look, including Heather Lee.

"Wow, Ethan, you've got your dad's talent."

Ethan felt himself blush. "Thanks."

Vika stood silently for a few seconds, hands on her hips, chewing her lower lip.

"No way," she said. "Your dad did this for you."

Ethan shook his head. "I got no help from my dad," he said, which was the truth, but he still felt a prick of guilt.

"This looks like his stuff."

"Ask him yourself," Ethan challenged her.

That silenced her for a moment, and Ethan hoped she'd go away. Then she said, "Okay. Draw something right now. Draw your gorilla."

Ethan was too startled to reply, but Soren saved him.

"You think you can just order people around?" Soren said. He massaged Ethan's shoulders like Ethan was a boxer about to go into the ring. "My man here works better in private."

"Yeah, right," said Vika, and returned to her own table.

Meanwhile, back home, Inkling was bored with eating newspaper. All those dull words and numbers. All those grainy pictures of men in suits. Restlessly, he slid out from underneath Ethan's bed.

From the moment he'd sprung free of the sketchbook, Inkling felt like there was someplace he was supposed to go, something he was supposed to find. Something to do with paper and ink, maybe. It was important. He hoped he'd know when he found it.

From Ethan's bookcase, the smell of ink and paper beckoned to him, but as he slid closer, he caught a second, more pungent whiff from the desk. There were two drawers, and the smell came from the bottom one. Inkling slipped inside.

He'd never seen such a glorious jumble of color and movement. At first he could only stare, quivering at Ethan's giant heap of comics. Superheroes and monster classics, and some of the latest stuff from Soren—or really, Soren's brother, who had everything, even stuff that Dad didn't like Ethan reading because he said it was too violent.

Inkling couldn't resist a moment longer. He poured himself onto the pile, inhaling magentas and yellows, feasting on letters of all shapes and sizes. Oh, the glory of it all! Even though he was close to bursting, it took all his willpower to stop. He swirled up out of the drawer like a tornado and vaulted down to the floor.

He couldn't stay still. He had to move. Like a storm vortex, he spun himself outside into the hallway and up the wall.

He'd seen so many incredible things in those comics, and he suddenly longed for a shape of his own! He wanted to be huge and powerful like the creatures he'd just read about.

And then he spotted, hanging on the wall, Mr. Rylance's vintage *King Kong* movie poster.

• • •

After school, Ethan walked home with Soren, who was busy telling him about the quadcopter his brother, Barnaby, had just bought.

"He wants to add mechanical claws to it," Soren said breathlessly. "So you can pick stuff up. You could fly it downstairs, take a cookie, and fly it back upstairs. And it's super quiet. It's called a Phantom Hawk! Pretty amazing, huh? Ethan?"

Ethan was having trouble concentrating. "Yeah, that's super cool. So has he let you fly it?"

His friend's shoulders slumped. "Not yet. Soon, though."

Ethan let out a big breath. "Look, I know you can keep a secret, right?"

"Absolutely. I mean, I've seen a lot of things I shouldn't have." He paused. "I've seen things that really no one should see."

"Okay, well, I need to tell you something."

"You found a dead body."

"What? No! I—"

"You're an alien in human flesh."

"Will you just listen to me? The drawings for our project. I didn't do them."

Soren looked at him in genuine surprise. "Your dad didn't do them, did he?"

"No. But I had some help. Well, more than help, really."

"So who did it?"

"It's easiest if I show you."

"Does it involve a portal to another dimen—"

"You'll see when we get to my place!"

• • •

Two steps inside the house and Ethan stopped cold. It looked like a chimpanzee with a paintbrush in each hand had cartwheeled through the hallway. There were colorful zigzags and red lightning bolts. But no chimpanzee could have also written giant words like *BLAM!* and *KAPOW!* and *THUKKKK!*

Soren started giggling, but it was a nervous giggle. "There was a movie like this, when a guy goes berserk and, um . . ."

For a second Ethan wondered if his father had gone crazy, but then he thought, *Inkling.*

"Are you guys maybe redecorating?" Soren asked.

Ethan followed the colorful mess into the living room, then the kitchen and dining room, searching for any signs of movement.

"Inkling!" he whispered.

"Who's Inkling?" Soren asked, wide-eyed.

Ethan hurried back to the hallway, but froze when the bathroom door opened and Dad walked out.

His father looked straight at him. Ethan looked straight back. His father's eyes flicked to Soren. Soren stared back, a smile glued to his face. Ethan's heartbeats went *thumpa thump, clompa clomp,* counting down the seconds before his dad noticed the chaotic graffiti everywhere. But his oblivious father just grunted, walked back to his studio, and shut the door behind him.

Ethan breathed again and rushed into his bedroom—

And recoiled, because charging across the back wall was an enormous ape, beating its chest, throwing its head back and howling. It was, in fact, silent, but in Ethan's head he heard everything: the thump of a meaty fist, the bloodcurdling wail.

"What the—!" exclaimed Soren.

"Shush!" Ethan hissed, dragging him into the room and slamming the door.

"What. Is. That?" Soren squeaked, because the giant gorilla, its head scraping the ceiling, was marching across the wall by the bed, straight toward them.

"Inkling!" Ethan said. "Stop it!"

The gorilla paused, then roared silently once more. A speech bubble expanded from his mouth, and inky words wrote themselves in spiky letters:

WHY SHOULD I, YOU PUNY LITTLE HUMAN?

Soren just stared.

I AM KONG, DREADED KING OF THE JUNGLE!

As if to demonstrate, a little biplane appeared from the shadow of Inkling's back and circled around his head. He pulverized it with a mighty fist.

"Inkling, you've got to clean up!" Ethan told him.

GIVE ME ONE GOOD REASON WHY I SHOULDN'T OBLITER-

"If my dad finds out about you, he'll put you back in his sketchbook!"

Ethan didn't know where this threat came from, but it did the trick.

NOT THE SKETCHBOOK, NO!!!

The giant ape collapsed like a burst balloon and fizzled back to a small splotch of ink on the wall.

"This is Inkling?" said Soren, staring.

"Yep."

"What is it?"

Ethan didn't know how to describe him properly: ink and energy and artistry and his father's imagination all mixed up in some kind of cauldron. Right now all he could worry about was getting the walls and ceiling cleaned up.

"The hallway," he said to Inkling. "Fast!"

While Soren listened outside Dad's studio, Ethan set Inkling on cleanup duty and watched as he surged over the walls, erasing and gathering the ink back into himself.

Ethan pointed at his father's vintage *King Kong* poster, now just a blank rectangle on the wall. "You can redraw it, can't you?"

He remembered the way Inkling had been able to redraw his mother's photograph perfectly.

From the wooden frame, Inkling cleverly slid underneath the glass so he was right on the poster itself. Inkling made himself into a long line and slowly rolled across the paper, leaving an exact replica of the movie poster in his wake.

"Whoa!" said Soren.

Ethan frowned and looked at the poster. Something was missing. He cocked his head at Inkling. "The biplanes, too, Inkling. Come on, spit them out."

Reluctantly, Inkling coughed back up the biplanes that were zooming toward King Kong as he leaned out from the Empire State Building.

"Thank you," said Ethan. "Now the rest of the house."

Inkling was amazingly fast. He just soared over all his graffiti, on walls and ceilings, erasing it effortlessly. When he was finished, Ethan grabbed an old magazine from the coffee table and held it against the wall so Inkling could flow onto it. Ethan didn't even notice the extra weight. Inkling ricocheted around the edges of the cover, erasing it stroke by stroke.

"Why're you so excited, Inkling?" Ethan asked when he and Soren were back inside his bedroom.

I'VE BEEN READING!!! SO MUCH ACTION!!! AND COLOR!!!

"What've you been reading?" Ethan asked. He had a suspicion.

COMICS!!!

Ethan opened his bottom desk drawer and peered inside at the massacred covers. He picked a few comics up and riffled through them, seeing the half-eaten pages.

"Oh, geez, that's one of my brother's," Soren said.

"It was a candy factory to Inkling," Ethan said. "At least it taught him to speak in full sentences."

On the magazine cover, Inkling was still bouncing around like a pinball.

"Okay, I don't think comics are good for you, Inkling."

NO, NO, NO! VERY GOOD! THEY'RE VERY GOOD!!!

"You need to calm down!"

Ethan went to the shelf and grabbed an old-looking book called *Anne of Green Gables*. His mother had given it to him, but he'd never read it because it was set in the past and was about a girl, so he assumed it must be boring. "Here, try this," he said.

Inkling eagerly glided onto the first page and started erasing the type line by line.

"Ethan," Soren said. "Where did you find . . . him?"

"He came from my father's sketchbook."

He told Soren everything.

"So let me get this straight," Soren said, watching as Inkling moved across the book's pages. "He eats whatever he touches."

"Yeah. Words, pictures. That's how he learned to read and draw. He can copy anything."

"How about TV or . . ." Soren pulled out his phone and opened up a picture of a beach with palm trees. He put it down on the book in front of Inkling. "Can you eat this, Inkling?"

Inkling bumped up against the phone and pulled back as

if surprised. On the bottom margin of the page he wrote:

**PLEASE DON'T INTERRUPT ME! I'M UTTERLY ENRAP-
TURED BY THIS GLORIOUS STORY!**

"Why's he talking like that?" Soren asked.

IT IS TRULY SUBLIME!

"I think he talks like whatever he's reading," Ethan said. "Inkling, we were just wondering if you could take a look at this picture."

Reluctantly, Inkling became a splotch again and flowed onto the screen of Soren's phone. Too late, he discovered it was the same slippery stuff that covered the posters in the hallway. Inkling skated helplessly across the glass, but the image of the beach didn't disappear or fade at all, even as he ricocheted back and forth a few times before hauling himself off the phone.

"He can't do screens!" Soren said.

"Ink," said Ethan. "Maybe it has to be ink!"

"Did you see anything, Inkling?" Soren asked.

Eagerly, Inkling flowed back onto the pages of the book, then wrote:

**I SAW NOTHING BUT A GREAT, ACHING DARKNESS.
IT WAS HORRID. PLEASE, I BEG YOU, NEVER PUT ME ON
SUCH A TERRIBLE THING AGAIN!**

Ethan smiled as Inkling happily continued reading, erasing word after word.

"So, he's the one who did our drawings?" Soren asked.

Ethan nodded.

"Why didn't you just tell us you couldn't draw?"

"Because you all thought I was some kind of genius! *I cannot draw!*"

It felt good to finally admit it.

"I can't hit a baseball," said Soren with a shrug. "Big deal. So. You just tell Inkling what to draw and he draws it?"

"I didn't need to, really. He read your story, and used my stick figures as a guide, and did the rest. It's cheating, right?"

He watched Soren, waiting for his reaction.

"I don't know. I mean, I saw Darren tracing stuff right off his phone. What's the difference?"

Ethan nodded. "Yeah! And did you see Susan H's character? It's a total copy of Spider-Man!"

"Exactly! And it's not like you're doing nothing. You rough in every panel with stick figures, right? And decide where the speech bubbles go. You're basically storyboarding the whole thing."

"I mean, I could rip up that first spread and start over by myself . . . ," Ethan said.

"No, no, no," said Soren. "Pino and Brady have already started the coloring and lettering."

"That's true," said Ethan. "It wouldn't be fair to them."

"Not fair at all," Soren agreed. "You going to tell your dad?"

Ethan shook his head. "Not yet. And you can't tell anyone either, okay? Not Pino or Brady."

"Of course not!" Soren agreed. "Can I see him draw?"

"Sure. Hey, Inkling, would you mind drawing a bit for us?"

Inkling paused, and his sides rose and fell in what looked like a dreamy sigh.

I FEEL LIKE I'VE JUST MADE A GREAT FRIEND!

"I'm glad you like the book," Ethan said. "Maybe I should read it."

I URGE YOU TO! ARE WE FRIENDS, ETHAN?

It was the first time Inkling had used his name, and Ethan felt a surprise wave of happiness. "Yeah, sure, we're friends," he replied.

He took hold of the book to carry Inkling over to his desk. When Inkling flowed right onto his hand, he gave a small gasp. Inkling had never touched him before. He stared at the black splotch on his skin. It felt like almost nothing. Was it a bit cooler? Yes, a little bit like a light breeze.

I WANT A CLOSER LOOK AT YOU, Inkling wrote on his hand.

And then he seeped up Ethan's sweatshirt all the way to his shoulder. Ethan stood very still, watching. Years ago, at an eco-reserve, a parrot had perched on him, and he felt the same nervous wonder now.

Like a cool gust of wind, Inkling slid onto his neck. Ethan hardly dared breathe. He felt like he was being explored. It was strange to think of himself as something alien, but he supposed he was to Inkling. Ethan walked over to the chest of drawers so he could watch in the mirror as Inkling flowed up over his jaw, past his ear, and across his forehead. It was a little unsettling seeing a big black splotch at the top of his face. He shivered a little.

Inkling slid down his nose and paused at the bottom, covering his nostrils. Ethan couldn't inhale, but before he could say anything, Inkling slid down over his mouth, too. His mouth was open, but Inkling's body was like a black film, stopping air from coming in or going out.

"Ethan?" Soren said worriedly. "You okay?"

Panicking, Ethan slapped at Inkling. The ink seemed to understand and quickly bolted off his face, down his arm to the chest of drawers.

"I couldn't breathe!" Ethan panted.

I AM SO SORRY, ETHAN!

"You can't just go covering people's noses and mouths!"

I DIDN'T KNOW! I WOULD NEVER HURT YOU!

"It's okay. It was an accident." Ethan believed him, but he looked at Inkling with a new respect and a bit of fear. Inkling wasn't just a magical blob of drawing ink; he was powerful. If he'd wanted to, Inkling could've suffocated him.

PLEASE FORGIVE ME. I AM IN THE DEPTHS OF DESPAIR!

Ethan couldn't help smiling. "It's okay, honest. You don't have to be in the depths of despair!"

He looked over at Soren, who had taken several steps back from Inkling.

"It's okay," Ethan told his unblinking friend.

"Is it? I mean, we don't really know what else he's capable of. Who knows what kind of dimension he came from? My brother would know. He's in high school—he knows about all sorts of stuff like this. We could ask him—"

"No," said Ethan. He was already starting to wonder if he should've told Soren. "No one else needs to know."

"You trust him?" Soren asked, nodding at Inkling.

"Absolutely. Inkling, are you ready to do another spread?"

MY HEART THRILLS AT THE IDEA!

Ethan carried him over to the desk, where a fresh piece of illustration board waited.

"Wait till you see this," he told Soren.

CHAPTER 6

At night, when everyone was asleep, Inkling explored some more.

Along the shadowy hallway, he slid cautiously, keeping an eye out for Rickman, who also kept night hours. To Inkling, the entire house smelled of ink and paper, especially the studio at the end of the hall. Was what he was searching for in there?

During the day, Inkling avoided that room—and Mr. Rylance. The sketchbook was there. And Inkling hated that sketchbook. It wanted to drag him back in. It was angry and sad—and Inkling sensed that Mr. Rylance was angry and sad, too. Still, the studio tugged at him.

He was getting closer when Rickman stepped out through the doorway and paused, ears pricked. Inkling shrank back against the baseboard. He feared that fiendish cat almost as much as the sketchbook. He hated the way his sharp claws could pierce him—and even though Inkling could just flow around them, and the little rips healed instantly, they still caused him pain.

Rickman sniffed the air. Inkling quickly retreated and slipped into the nearest room. He didn't want to stay too near the door, in case the cat came in, so he moved closer to the bed. Mr. Rylance was snoring. He moved around the clothes dumped on the floor and climbed the leg of a night table. On top was a phone, a book, and a tumbler that held the sticky remnants of a strong-smelling liquid.

Mr. Rylance turned over in his sleep, bringing his face within inches of the night table.

Inkling was startled to find himself suddenly drawing. He didn't seem to have any control over it. One of his inky tendrils was frantically sketching on the table: faces, rooms, everyday things—all so quickly that he was drawing one thing over the other, as if trying to keep up with . . . with what?

He realized he must somehow be *seeing* Mr. Rylance's dreams. Except that he wasn't even seeing them—he was just drawing whatever was circling around in Mr. Rylance's sleeping head.

For the first time, Inkling understood that he hadn't just come from Mr. Rylance's sketchbook; he'd come from Mr. Rylance *himself*.

How else could he be frantically sketching his dreams?

Suddenly there was a bed.

This was important—more so than the things he'd already sketched. Why was it so familiar? Yes, he'd drawn a bit of it, that time when he'd been doodling and Ethan had walked in and seen him. It was an unusual bed, with high sides and a railing around it. It had a green blanket—nasty color—over it, and from the ridges and wrinkles it was clear there was someone lying underneath.

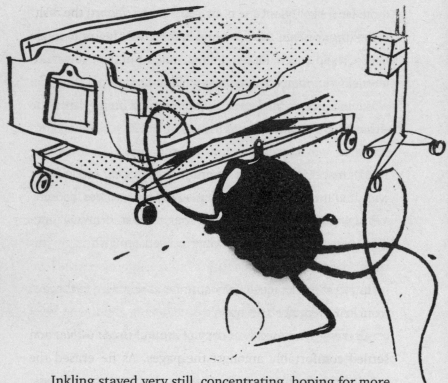

Inkling stayed very still, concentrating, hoping for more of the picture to come. But at that moment, Rickman jumped up onto the bottom of the bed and glared right at Inkling.

Fast, Inkling erased his drawings and slid down to the carpet. He made a dash for the door. Behind him, he heard

Rickman land heavily. Into the hallway Inkling bolted and pressed himself flat against the baseboard. He knew he had a few seconds and shaped himself into a dish, same as the one he'd seen Rickman eating from.

Rickman emerged from the room, and his eyes locked onto the dish against the wall. His dish was *never* there. And yet, it was undeniably a dish, and in a dish there was usually food. He forgot about the hunt and padded toward the dish.

Inkling watched him coming closer. Over the past couple of days, he'd done a lot of reading, and one of the things he'd learned was what cats were most afraid of. When Rickman was just a few inches away, Inkling swirled himself into the shape of a cobra and sprang like something from a jack-in-the-box.

Rickman lifted straight up off the floor, ricocheted off the wall, and hurled himself down the hallway into the kitchen.

Inkling formed himself into a happy face on the wall and jiggled around a bit. That was *very* satisfying, but he was tired now. He slid back to Ethan's room. Underneath the bed, he found a blank piece of newsprint and sketched the image from Peter Rylance's dream.

Afterward, he found his copy of *Anne of Green Gables* and settled comfortably amongst the pages. As he erased the words, it wasn't because he was hungry anymore; he just wanted to read. It was the pure enjoyment of being told a story before bedtime. He read many pages, each one more slowly than the last, before he finally slowed to a halt and was still.

Ethan woke up to a flashlight shining directly into his eyes and a small hand joggling his shoulder.

"She is sorry to disturb you," Sarah whispered.

"What're you doing?" Ethan said, pushing the flashlight to one side.

"Are you awake, Ethan?"

"I am now!"

"Where is Lucy?"

With a sigh, Ethan sat up and looked at his bedside clock. It wasn't so bad. His alarm was set to go off in ten minutes anyway.

From underneath the bed, Inkling bounded out in the shape of a puppy.

"Lucy!" said Sarah. "You came back! We were so worried about you!"

Inkling capered around on the floor, and Sarah giggled with delight. A speech bubble appeared from his mouth, and inside was the word:

WOOF!

"She said *woof!*" Sarah exclaimed. "She is a very clever puppy."

"She sure is," Ethan agreed.

No one saw Rickman enter Ethan's room. Rickman was not the smartest cat in the world, but he was fairly sure that the inky puppy on the floor was somehow connected to the inky thing that had scared him half to death last night. Now he wanted revenge. He wanted to catch something just once in his life. He prowled closer, then pounced.

The moment Rickman's claws sank into Inkling, the puppy collapsed into a small, terrified blob. Inkling poured around Rickman's claws and bolted across the room. Rickman pounced again, missed. By this time, Inkling was out into the hallway.

"Icklan!" hollered Sarah. "You naughty cat! You have hurt Lucy!"

Ethan dashed after the cat and scooped him up. Rickman twisted for a few seconds, and even showed his teeth, but Ethan looked stern and puffed air on him, and the cat eventually went boneless. It wasn't worth all this effort. He was old, after all. Food didn't have to be so much work. Maybe he'd try again when he had a better chance.

Ethan looked around the hallway but couldn't see Inkling anywhere.

"Inkling," he called softly.

"Lucy!" Sarah shouted.

Obviously, Inkling was scared enough to go into hiding for a while, but Ethan wasn't happy. What if he decided to make an appearance in front of Dad?

As if on cue, Dad zombie-walked into the hallway.

"So . . . all right, let's . . . ," he said, and disappeared into the washroom.

As Ethan got dressed, he checked in the most likely places for Inkling, without luck. There was nothing he could do right now. He had to help Sarah pick out her clothes (which took a long time because she had very strong opinions about her wardrobe), then start the coffee machine going and set the table for breakfast. Mom had never asked him to do all these things, but Dad expected him to help more.

He looked around the hallway one last time, but still no sign of Inkling. Ethan figured he'd just have to hope Inkling stayed hidden.

• • •

When Ms. D left the classroom during their work period, Vika walked over to Ethan's table and stood with her hands on her hips, gazing at their new spread. Pino was coloring some of the panels, and Brady was inking in the lettering— more neatly than anyone had expected.

"Pretty great work," said Vika, nodding.

Ethan looked at her carefully, not sure whether she was being sincere.

"You guys should have a look at this," Vika said to the class. "It's amazing."

"Thanks!" said Brady, who liked everyone, including Vika.

Ethan started to feel nervous. Heather Lee and a bunch of other kids came over to have a closer look.

"But you know what's weird?" said Vika pleasantly. "I've never seen Ethan actually draw anything in this classroom. Not a single thing."

"He works better at home," Soren said.

"True," said Ethan, feeling sweaty.

"Makes me wonder if you work at all," she said.

"Get lost, Vika," Ethan retorted, but he watched her

nervously, especially her right leg, that same leg that had tornado-kicked him into the garbage can.

"And look," Vika said, "you don't even have any ink on your fingers." She held up her own hands so everyone could see the smudges. "If you draw, you get inky."

"Maybe I just wash my hands better than you," Ethan retorted, and some kids laughed. Vika was right, though. His fingers were totally unstained. His dad's were never this clean. He should've thought of that and dabbed some marker on them.

Vika just smiled at her friend Sandra and said, "Told you." The two girls shared a knowing smirk.

Ethan looked around at his classmates, and Heather. They were all watching him. Did they think his father had done the artwork? He wanted to erase that smirk on Vika's face.

"You want to see me draw?" he said rashly.

"Ethan," said Soren, putting a nervous hand on his shoulder, "she's not the boss of you. You don't need to—"

"No, let's do it!" said Ethan, glaring at Vika.

"Awesome!" said Vika, and she slapped a blank piece of paper down in front of him. "Go for it!"

Ethan grabbed his fine-tipped black marker. He'd been watching Inkling draw their gorilla character over and over. He could probably do a pretty good copy.

But when he uncapped his marker and touched the point to the paper, he realized how much trouble he was in. What was he doing? He couldn't draw anything!

"Oh, man," squeaked Soren.

"Come on!" sneered Vika. "Draw!"

At first, Ethan thought that the black dot growing from the tip of his pen was just the marker bleeding into the paper. But then he saw the dot give a familiar shimmer and lean just a little bit in one direction. Inkling! Quickly, Ethan moved his pen the same way. The bead of ink kept going, just a smidge ahead of the tip of his pen. Ethan kept pace.

Inkling was on his pen! Ethan didn't know how, and he didn't care. Inkling sped up and Ethan matched him, hardly daring to blink in case he slipped too far behind and someone noticed that the gorilla was drawing itself.

"You're so fast!" he heard Heather Lee say, and his heart gave a happy squeeze.

Ethan felt like he was in a trance. He wasn't even seeing the gorilla take shape because all his attention was on the line that was seeping away from his pen, moving, moving—

And then suddenly stopped. Ethan inhaled sharply and lifted his hand from the paper.

"Gorilla!" he proclaimed, and saw the picture in front of him for the first time. He tried not to look amazed, because it was truly fantastic.

"That's incredible!" Heather said.

A few people actually clapped. Someone gave him a high five.

"Way to go, buddy!" said Soren, whose eyes were still wide with terror. He looked around at everyone defiantly. "See what my boy did?"

"You can apologize anytime now!" Pino said to Vika, who was staring from the drawing to Ethan, her eyes narrowed meanly.

Ethan looked around. He felt fantastic. This must be how his father felt all those times people clapped for him in bookstores and conventions! He could see the admiration in everyone's eyes—and the brightest were Heather Lee's.

"That was amazing, Ethan," she said.

"What's going on?" Ms. D said, coming back into the room.

Everyone scattered to their own tables.

"You're supposed to be working with your groups. Come on, guys, you aren't in kindergarten. Let's focus! Back to work, please."

Vika gave Ethan one last suspicious look and turned away.

• • •

Ethan wasn't the only one giddy with triumph. Inkling was revved up, too. He'd never drawn for an audience before, and he liked the applause and cheering. He'd wanted to keep going. He would've done all sorts of fabulous things. But Ethan had already lifted the pen away from the paper.

Inkling quickly moved into the shadows of Ethan's palm, then up his wrist and onto the sleeve of his dark sweater. Inkling made himself thin as thread and weaved his way up the arm, then back down toward Ethan's jeans pocket, where he'd spent most of the morning, peeping out and taking everything in.

After Rickman had attacked him earlier that morning, he'd found the perfect hiding place in Ethan's backpack.

There was even a good book inside, called *The BFG,* to keep him occupied. Plus, he got a trip outside the house! He was seeing all sorts of new things.

Just as Inkling was about to slip back inside Ethan's pocket, he glimpsed Soren's sneakers. They were the brightest red he'd ever seen, brighter even than comic-book red—and he wanted it. He couldn't help himself. He poured himself down the seam of Ethan's jeans. There were lots of feet down here, all restlessly squeaking and nudging the gritty floor. A quick slither and Inkling was on Soren's left shoe.

He surged across the canvas sides first, trying to absorb every last drop of that delicious red. But nothing was happening. The red stayed on the shoe. What Inkling didn't know was that dye was an entirely different thing from ink. In consternation, Inkling swerved to the top of the shoe, but that red also stayed fixed in place.

He was about to try Soren's other shoe when the lunch bell rang. Instantly, everyone was on their feet, and chair legs were being pushed around, and Soren was walking.

Inkling thought it best just to hold on for the moment.

• • •

Ethan, meanwhile, was panicking. Where was Inkling? He'd lost track of him after they finished the gorilla drawing. While his friends packed up their backpack, Ethan poked his hands into all his pockets, hoping to feel the gusty chill of Inkling. He looked on his chair, his clothing. Down on his hands and knees, he checked the floor. He wanted to call out but was worried someone would overhear.

"Lose something?" Vika asked, walking past him.

Then he saw Soren's shoes, one red, one with a big black moving splotch on it.

Ethan hurried after his friend into the hallway.

"That was incredible in there," Soren said when Ethan caught up. "You didn't tell me you brought him to school!"

"I didn't know," said Ethan. "And he's on your shoe. Don't stop, just keep going."

Soren glanced down and gulped. "I don't know how I feel about this, Ethan. What if he decides to . . . climb up?"

Ethan looked around nervously. The lunchtime hallway was noisy and crowded and he doubted anyone would notice, but he wanted to go somewhere quiet, fast.

"I'm freaking out a little, Ethan."

"Don't freak out, okay? We'll go to the bathroom."

"I'm freaking out! What if he swarms up my face!"

Without warning, Inkling darted off Soren's shoe, dodging around people's feet, and slid right underneath the door of the art room.

Ethan rushed over and tried the knob. The door was locked.

CHAPTER 7

I t was the smell that had lured Inkling inside. How could he resist? The room positively blossomed with the scent of ink. Inkling followed it up onto a long table. Spread out in a row were dozens of pieces of paper. And on each was a huge splotch of black ink.

He froze, stunned. He'd never dreamed there were others like him!

He'd thought he was alone in the wide world.

Was this what he was supposed to find? A place with creatures like him?

Inkling raced to the nearest piece of paper. He wanted to touch the other ink splotch, but he thought that might be rude, so instead he wrote:

GREETINGS!

No reply. Inkling tried again, using the language he'd just learned from his latest book.

I IS INKLING. WHO IS YOU?

Again, not a flicker of response.

YOU IS VERY UNFRIENDSOME, he wrote, and moved on to the next splotch, which was shaped like a crooked butterfly.

HELLO! YOU IS LOOKING LIKE A WHOPSY BUTTER-FLAPPER!

Nothing. This time Inkling reached out with a tendril and politely tapped the other splotch. It didn't move. Inkling nudged harder, and the part of the butterfly he touched just disappeared, slurped up inside him.

Inkling backed off. With a squeeze of loneliness, he realized these were not creatures like him at all. They were just drawings, just ordinary bits of lifeless ink.

He had no way of knowing that this was the work of second graders learning about action art. Some had splattered their paper with ink from a brush. Others had punched ink onto their paper with sponges. And still others had dripped ink onto one half of the paper, folded, squished, and unfolded it to see what pattern they'd made.

Inkling rested for a moment, and his disappointment turned to annoyance.

These pictures weren't very good. They were messy. They didn't look like anything at all—well, except that butterfly one.

Inkling figured he might as well improve things a bit. He'd seen (and eaten) enough pictures by now to have lots of ideas. He got to work. The first ink splotch he turned into a picture of the moon with all its pockmarks and ridges. The second, a volcano exploding. Another splotchy mess he expertly transformed into a fireworks display against a city skyline.

He was so involved in what he was doing that he didn't notice the lights coming on and people entering the room.

• • •

"Thanks, Mr. Sawyer," Ethan said. "I left my study notes in here, and my test is next period."

"Hurry, please," said the art teacher. "I've got a class coming in two minutes."

Ethan and Soren started looking. What Ethan saw was a room full of paper and canvases and brushes and artwork. A million places where Inkling could hide—and eat himself into something the size of the *Titanic*.

"Wow, those are really good," Soren said, pointing at the ink drawings on the table.

"Yes," said Mr. Sawyer, "those are the second graders' . . ." He stepped closer and frowned. "But that's not what we were doing. How did these . . ."

Ethan's eyes skated across the ink drawings and skidded to a halt at the last one. Because this one was moving. All the splotchy bits were shaping themselves into a horse rearing up on its hind legs.

He put himself between the picture and Mr. Sawyer.

"Maybe the ink just kind of soaked into the paper and got

all smeared," said Ethan helpfully. He backed up until he bumped against the table. With one hand he reached back until he felt the edges of the paper Inkling was on.

"No," said Mr. Sawyer, "I don't see how this is possible. . . ."

Ethan coughed and whipped the paper off the table, keeping it behind him. Mr. Sawyer didn't notice. Leaning over another drawing, he peered closer.

"I think these kids are all really talented!" said Soren, understanding what was going on. "You're doing a great job, Mr. Sawyer!"

Ethan glanced at the paper in his hand to make sure Inkling was still on it, happily drawing away. He folded it up and crammed it into his pocket.

"Strangest thing," muttered Mr. Sawyer.

Ethan grabbed Soren by the sleeve and started dragging him out of the room.

"Thanks, Mr. Sawyer!" said Ethan.

The teacher looked up. "What about your study notes?"

"I must've left them somewhere else."

Ethan marched to the bathroom with Soren. There was no one else inside. He pulled the paper from his pocket and unfolded it. Inkling shimmered.

"You can't just take off like that!" Ethan said to him.

I IS HAVING A FROTHSOME ADVENTURE!

"He's talking all weird again," Soren said.

"Inkling, are you by any chance reading—"

THE WHIZZPOPPING BOOK IN YOUR KNACKERSACK!

Ethan burst out laughing. "*The BFG!* That's exactly the way he talks! But, Inkling, why'd you run away from us?"

I THOUGHT THERE WERE OTHERS. BUT THEY WERE JUST SLOTHSOME INK.

It took Ethan a second to understand. "Yeah, just drawings."

I AM ALONESOME.

Without knowing what he was doing, he patted Inkling— the same way he patted Sarah to reassure her after she tripped. It just seemed like the thing to do.

"Well, you're not really alonesome, because you have me," Ethan said. "And I was worried I'd lost you. Please don't run off again."

Inkling formed into a smiley face.

"I didn't even know you were in my backpack!"

I WAS HIDING FROM THAT FANGDOODLE RICKMAN.

"Well, I'm glad you did, because I couldn't have drawn that gorilla alone!"

YOU IS WELCOME. THAT HUMAN BEAN, VIKA, SHE IS A FILTHSOME KIDDLE.

Ethan couldn't help laughing. "I agree."

I CAN GOBBLEFUNK HER DRAWINGS IF YOU LIKE.

"What? No, no, that's okay. You're helping me enough already." He sighed. "Way too much." The bell rang, and he started folding up the paper again. "I'm putting you back in my pocket now."

He and Soren left the washroom and headed to class.

"Inkling's pretty amazing," Soren said. "The way he can just draw anything."

"And not just pictures," Ethan said. "He can write—he remembers any word he erases."

Soren was quiet a moment, then said, "Hey, do you think Inkling would mind if I borrowed him?"

Ethan glanced over in surprise. "What for?"

"The history test next week. Inkling could read all my notes and then, you know, rewrite the answers for me."

"Are you serious?"

There was a tangle of feelings in his head, but the strongest was that he absolutely did not want to share Inkling. He didn't want Soren taking him home, or holding him, or even talking to him. Inkling was something special that belonged only to him, Ethan.

"I can never remember all those dates," Soren was saying. "It's not my fault I have a lousy memory! What do you say?"

"But it's cheating," Ethan replied before he could stop himself.

Soren looked genuinely hurt for a second and then muttered, "How's it any different from what you're doing?"

Ethan scowled and kicked an empty drink box across the floor. Then he sighed and said, "It's not."

• • •

"Inkling," Ethan said after school, "could you teach me how to draw?"

He was sitting at his desk, watching Inkling work on a new spread, transforming his penciled stick figures into beautiful images. He knew he'd never be good enough to do that.

He also knew that he wasn't going to throw out all the amazing work Inkling had already completed. Soren was absolutely right: he'd been cheating all along, and there was no point making excuses for himself. But maybe he could make it better by trying his hardest to learn, and draw as much of the graphic novel as possible.

Inkling wrote:

ABSOLUTELY! I CAN COACH YOU!

Since getting home, Inkling had made a snack of the sports section of the newspaper, and the way he talked had changed again.

"How should we do this?"

JUST DO IT! I WILL ASSIST.

Ethan uncapped his best marker, studying the next panel. In his imagination, he could picture it exactly.

PLAY TO WIN!

Ethan lowered his marker, and Inkling sent out a little tendril of ink to meet the tip as it touched the paper.

This time, Inkling let Ethan take the lead. Frowning in concentration, Ethan roughed in the gorilla, trying to get the overall shape and posture right, the angry scowl on the ape's face. He felt like everything he did was a mistake.

GET IN THE GAME, ETHAN!

"I'm doing my best!"

EYES ON THE PRIZE!

"It's kind of hard to concentrate with you talking like that."

I CAN BENCH THE PEP TALK.

As Ethan drew, Inkling would sometimes make whisker-thin lines to suggest a better way. If the mistakes were too big, and Ethan asked, Inkling erased them so he could take another try. Together they worked for twenty minutes, completely absorbed, and finished the panel.

When Ethan put the pen down, he was pleasantly surprised by what he'd drawn. Even with Inkling helping him every step of the way, it wasn't great. In no way was it great. But it was better than what he'd done several days ago.

GOOD WORK, TEAM!

"Thanks." He looked back at Inkling's previous panels. Despite the intentional smudges and messy bits, they were so much better than what he'd just done.

"People will know," he said, shaking his head. "They'll know someone else did it."

In a quick whirl of inky fingers, Inkling danced across Ethan's picture and left behind a much-improved drawing. It didn't have quite the polish of the earlier work, but it looked more consistent.

"I guess that's how we'll have to do it," Ethan said with a resigned sigh. "But I work first, okay? And then you can make it better—and maybe I'll improve as I go along."

OF COURSE YOU WILL!

It wasn't a perfect plan, but it was the best one Ethan could come up with right now. He was determined: he'd make the graphic novel as much of his own as humanly possible.

"Thanks again, Inkling. We'll do some more later, okay?"

· · ·

At dinner, Sarah couldn't stop talking about Lucy.

Sarah only talked in stories. If you asked her how she was, or what she did at school, she just looked at you like you were the most boring person in the world. What she wanted to talk about was her favorite TV shows and books, usually all mixed together, over and over again. Tonight, there was a new character at least: Lucy the puppy. Lucy was chased by mean dogs; Lucy got thorns in her paws; Lucy was lost and scared and needed rescuing.

Sarah's speech wasn't always clear, and when she got really excited, she held her hands in front of her and wiggled her fingers. Ethan was better at understanding her than Dad was, and he could tell Dad was getting frustrated by all the commotion.

"Who's Moosey?" Dad asked, pouring himself another glass of wine.

"*Lucy*. It's a puppy. On a show she likes," Ethan lied.

"Lucy is Sarah's puppy!" Sarah insisted.

"Is that your favorite show now?" Dad asked her.

"Dada, Lucy is not a show. She is a puppy!"

"Fine, okay," said Dad, rubbing the spot between his eyes, hard.

Sarah launched into a Lucy story she'd already told five minutes ago.

"I wouldn't mind just a few new stories," Dad muttered.

"They're based on her favorite TV episodes," Ethan explained. He'd heard them playing from the TV room so many times he could almost recite the lines and sing the songs.

"This is making me crazy," Dad said as Sarah prattled on. "It's like she's *stuck*."

Kind of like you, Ethan thought but didn't say.

"Maybe she watches too much TV," Ethan said instead.

Dad looked at him in annoyance. "Maybe you should play with her more, then."

"I do play with her! More than you!"

"You're a kid. Kids play. I've got to work."

Ethan held his tongue. Obviously Dad had had another bad day.

"Karl's dropping by later," Dad said.

"Carol!" Sarah shouted happily.

Carol was Sarah's babysitter, and Sarah adored her. Karl didn't sound so different from Carol, especially if you said them quickly.

"Not *Carol*," Ethan explained carefully. *"Karl."*

Sarah looked at him sternly. "Sarah is very disappointed."

It wasn't unusual for Dad's publisher to pop by, look at the latest artwork, have a drink. Not so much in the last couple of years, but when Dad was doing the Kren series, Karl Worthington often showed up with good news and a bottle of champagne to celebrate an award, or a bestseller list, or being translated into Korean.

Warily, Ethan asked, "Is Vika coming?"

"I think he said he's bringing her, yeah."

"Greaaaaaaat," said Ethan.

"You guys are still in the same class, right?" his father asked.

"Yes!" Ethan said. "We've been in the same class forever!"

"I thought you two could play with Sarah so Karl and I have a chance to talk."

Ethan breathed in, let it out. "Okay."

CHAPTER 8

When the doorbell rang, Sarah ran down the hallway, shouting, "Carol!" and was disappointed all over again when Dad opened the door and Karl and Vika were standing there.

Sarah squinted. She was a bit nearsighted.

"Let's try again," she said, trying to close the door on them, as if next time might be different.

Ethan disguised his laugh with a cough. This was exactly what he wished he could do to Vika.

But Dad stopped Sarah and ushered Karl and Vika inside.

"Sarah, you are so much taller!" Karl said. "How old are you?"

"She's nine!" Sarah answered.

"Not yet you aren't," Dad told her. "One more sleep."

"She's having a party!" Sarah said, and ran back to the TV room.

"Hi, Mr. Rylance," said Vika, pretending she was a normal person, smiling a normal smile.

"Hi, Vika. Nice to see you again."

"How's your latest book coming along?" Vika asked as they walked to the living room.

Ethan sighed inwardly. Vika didn't have a clue about living with an artist, especially one who was blocked.

"Great!" Dad said. "Very well!"

Ethan could hear the exclamation-mark lies in his voice. Vika and Karl must know anyway. If the work were going well, there'd be a new book to show, wouldn't there? Or at least new artwork.

"Great to hear!" said Karl. "Anything you could show?"

"Not yet. I want to wait till it's all finished and get a fresh reaction."

"Of course, absolutely."

It was weird watching adults lie to each other, Ethan thought. Dad was lying, and Karl knew he was lying, but everyone just kept pretending.

"Ethan's doing some amazing artwork at school," Vika said.

Ethan was horrified that Dad couldn't see her fake smile and the gleam from her archenemy teeth.

"Great," said Mr. Rylance distractedly.

"His style really takes after yours."

"Oh?" said Mr. Rylance, smiling vaguely at Ethan. Ethan had told Dad tons of times about the graphic novel project—and asked him for help!—but Dad had obviously forgotten the whole thing.

"They're doing graphic novels at school," Mr. Worthington said helpfully.

"Right, right," Dad said. "Two artists in the family, heaven help us."

"Have you seen it?" Vika persisted.

"No, Ethan hasn't shown it to me. But I'm glad it's going well. . . ."

Karl beamed at Ethan. "Taking after your old man, huh? I'll be signing *you* up next."

"You'll be signing *me* up next," Vika said firmly.

"Goes without saying," her dad replied.

"Hey, Ethan," said his father, "why don't you and Vika go watch some TV or something, keep an eye on Sarah."

"Sure," said Vika perkily. "Sounds great."

"Oh, and, Ethan," Dad added, "maybe Vika would like a drink of something."

"Uh-huh," he said, walking to the kitchen.

At the fridge, without looking at Vika, he asked, "What would you like to drink?" He sounded like the GPS in Dad's car.

"What do you have?"

He opened the fridge door, hating her. "There's cranberry juice."

"No thanks."

"Orange juice."

"No thanks."

"Milk."

"I'm lactose intolerant."

"Ginger ale."

"Do you have any lime water?"

"No."

"What were the choices again?"

"Cranberry, orange, milk—"

"Cranberry, please."

He poured her a glass of juice and held it out, his arm fully extended. She took the glass and had a long sip, watching him with narrowed eyes. Ethan walked to the TV room, where Sarah was standing right in front of the screen, watching two bad mice rip apart a doll's house.

"Those naughty mice!" she said, pointing, her mouth wide with feigned horror. There was nothing Sarah loved better than getting angry at animals. "Ethan, be angry with them!"

"You naughty mice!" Ethan shouted at the TV.

Vika giggled. "She's super cute."

Ethan sat down on the sofa.

"What's her name?" Sarah asked him, pointing at Vika.

Sarah had met Vika many times before, but she liked to be reminded of people's names.

"Vika," Ethan said.

"Eeka," Sarah said, walking over and taking her hand. "Be angry at the mice!"

"They're terrible mice!" said Vika.

Rickman, looking for love, wandered into the room and somehow managed to heave himself up onto the television console. He flopped down in front of the screen, purring and offering himself to be stroked.

"Icklan! Off!" said Sarah, and pushed the cat.

Rickman landed on the carpet with as much dignity as his aged limbs allowed. With a flick of his tail, he left the room.

"Why doesn't she like the cat?" Vika asked Ethan.

Ethan shrugged.

"Icklan scratched Sarah," Sarah told Vika.

This was news to Ethan. "Really?"

Sarah rolled up her sleeve and showed Vika. There was no mark there.

"Hmm," she said. "Must've been a long time ago."

Ethan wondered if this was truth or story. Either way, he was annoyed she'd told Vika instead of him. Not even Sarah recognized that Vika was evil. For the next five minutes, Vika and Sarah talked about the TV show. Then Sarah introduced her to all her favorite toy dogs.

"Where's your washroom?" Vika asked.

"Just turn right," Ethan said.

After she left, Ethan walked down the hallway so he could listen, out of sight, to his father and Karl in the living room. He heard the sound of wine being poured.

". . . sales of Kren are really slowing down, but I know they'd come roaring back if we had a new title in the series."

"What can I tell you, Karl. It's just not in the works."

"Okay, that's cool. But you really need to get something out there. You're two years over deadline."

"I know, I know."

"The money from Kren isn't going to last forever," Karl said, then added more quietly, "and you've got your kids to think about."

Ethan's heart counted down the beats to his father's terse reply:

"We're fine."

"Hey, there's something I wanted to show you," Karl said. "Maybe you've already seen it."

Ethan leaned out around the corner to see Karl handing a comic to Dad.

"*Exterminatrix,*" Dad said, looking at the cover. "This one of yours?"

"I wish. This thing is selling in the millions. People are nuts about it. It's definitely not for kids."

"So I see," Dad said, riffling through the pages. Ethan could tell he didn't like what he was seeing, just by the shape of his mouth. "Wow, this is super violent stuff. It's all exploding heads. Plus, the artwork's ugly."

"I know. It's trash," said Karl. "But you could do something like this in your sleep. We both know that."

"Not my kind of thing."

"Unfortunately, it's the kind of thing a lot of people want right now."

Dad handed it back to Karl. "I think you'll like what I'm working on. I'm very close."

Another total lie, Ethan thought.

"Well, that is good news. Any idea when you'll be finished?"

"Nine months, tops."

"Can you make it four?"

Ethan gulped.

"With a bit of luck, sure," Dad said.

"Okay, well, cheers to that," said Karl. They lifted their glasses and clinked. "Can't wait to see it. I'm sure it's going to be every bit as successful as Kren."

Ethan felt his heart tumble inside his chest. He retreated to the TV room and sat down beside Sarah, who automatically threw a soft arm around his shoulder—like she knew exactly what he needed.

Dad hadn't started anything. He didn't even have an *idea.* And all that stuff Karl had said about sales of Kren slowing down. Did that mean they were running out of money, too? What would happen then?

"Where is Eeka?" Sarah asked him suddenly.

Ethan frowned. "That," he said, "is a very good question."

• • •

Just one page, Inkling told himself.

He knew he shouldn't, but he couldn't help it. The newspaper under the bed was so dull and dry and left such a gritty afterimage. It was books he liked best—they were more nutritious and they lasted longer inside him. But . . . but color was good, too. If he could just have a *little* color, he'd be all right.

Stealthily, Inkling slunk out from underneath the bed and made his way to Ethan's desk. He slipped into the comic drawer and—

Oh! The ecstasy! One page turned into two, turned into ten as Inkling inhaled the colors, the words. It was a feast of heroes and villains, machines and magic. There was shouting and punching and explosions. People jumped and flew. They crushed things. They didn't just hide under beds.

Inkling wanted to move, too. He couldn't help it. He wanted to be as big as his noisy thoughts.

He slid out of the drawer to the floor and climbed the wall like some mutant vine, spreading tendrils, stretching into a witchy black tree. The branches lashed about in a gale, but that wasn't enough for Inkling, so he formed himself into a giant robot warrior, floor to ceiling, and went stomping back and forth across the wall behind Ethan's desk—

Just as the door opened and Vika crept into the room.

Inkling froze midstride, like some enormous piece of graffiti. It was really quite magnificent: a robot bristling with weapons and antennae, taking up the whole wall and the curtains, which rustled slightly in the breeze of the door opening, so that it looked like the robot's chest fluttered with a steel heartbeat.

Vika stared at Inkling, impressed.

"Cool," she said to herself.

She moved straight for Ethan's desk, where the latest spread of the graphic novel rested. A few more panels had been added since what she'd seen today at school.

She'd already been to Mr. Rylance's studio, hoping she'd find the graphic novel on *his* drafting table—because then she could take a picture with her phone and have proof that Ethan's dad was doing all his work. But there'd been nothing there, except his sketchbook, which she'd looked through a tiny bit, just because his work was so amazing and she hoped, one day, she'd be half as good as Peter Rylance.

Now here she was in Ethan's bedroom, and there was the graphic novel on his desk, like he'd done it himself. Except that he couldn't have. She just knew. It was way too good.

From the wall, Inkling watched Vika. There was a mean look on her face. Was she going to do something to the drawings?

Inkling was ready for action.

Slowly, he started to change shape.

• • •

Ethan burst into the room and Vika whirled guiltily to face him.

"What're you doing?" he demanded.

She shrugged. "Just checking out your room."

"Yeah, well, get out!"

"Fine!" She started walking.

Behind her, Ethan saw Inkling morph into a terrifying

giant squid thing, lashing its tentacles and jetting around the walls toward the door. A speech bubble inflated from its jagged, beaked mouth and spelled out the word:

SHHHHHLUUUUURKKK!

Desperately, Ethan shook his head, and before he could stop himself, he shouted:

"Don't!"

Vika looked at him strangely. "Don't what? I'm leaving, all right?"

"Yeah, go ahead," said Ethan, his eyes still on Inkling.

Vika must have seen him staring because she turned. Inkling froze. Vika frowned at the huge squid on the wall beside her. Then she looked at the now-blank wall behind Ethan's desk.

"There used to be a mural there," she said, pointing.

"Hmm?" said Ethan.

"A robot thing. It was huge."

Ethan pursed his lips. "No."

From the corner of his eye, he saw Inkling lift a tentacle, like he meant to flail out at Vika. Ethan tilted his head warningly.

Vika started to turn back to the squid thing, and at that exact moment, Inkling decided to pour himself off the wall.

"Where'd it go?" Vika cried.

"What?" said Ethan.

She walked over, touched the wall, then peered down at the floor. A small, dark puddle lapped against the baseboard.

"What is that?" Vika said, reaching out with her hand.

"Just some old paint," Ethan answered lamely.

The moment Vika touched Inkling, he surged onto her hand, then over her shirt, faster than a cockroach. With a shriek, Vika staggered back and tripped. Inkling raced round and round her body.

"Get it off me!" she hollered.

"Get what off you?" Ethan asked as Inkling made himself very small and darted onto Vika's back.

She jerked round, trying to look over her shoulder, but Inkling was faster, and just kept zipping out of sight.

"Is it on me?" she gasped.

"There's nothing on you, Vika."

He patted her on the back, and Inkling flowed onto his hand and slipped out of sight.

"There's something weird going on," Vika said, getting up. She looked completely shaken, but also angry. For a second Ethan worried she might tornado-kick him.

"You guys okay?" his father called out from the living room.

"Yeah, fine!" Vika called back. "I just tripped."

Ethan expected her to go running now. But she stared hard at him.

"What is it?" she demanded.

"What's what?"

"It's some weird . . . robot or something. That's what's been drawing for you."

Ethan let out a big breath. "I have a confession to make."

"About time!"

"They're aliens."

She shoved past him. "Very funny."

"Better tell Ms. D tiny aliens are doing my drawings," Ethan said as she left his room.

And then he went to his bed and let Inkling slip away underneath.

CHAPTER 9

"I forgot the cake," Dad said. "I'm just going to run to the bakery and get it."

"What?" Ethan said, horrified. "You can't leave me alone with them!"

Hurling themselves around the living room were six little kids who'd just been dropped off for Sarah's birthday party. Four were girls from school, and the other two were from Sarah's special-needs playgroup.

"Twenty minutes, tops," Dad said. "I also have to get stuff for the piñata."

"You forgot the piñata stuff, too?"

"I thought it came with stuff already inside! There's a dollar store near the bakery—I'll just buy a whole bunch of crap."

"I don't think I'm ready for this!" Ethan protested.

"I'll be fast. It's not a big deal—just get them interested in that."

He pointed to the easel he'd set up. At birthday parties, Dad always drew for the kids. They'd shout out what they wanted, and he'd do it. Things got added to the drawing, and pretty soon it would turn into a kind of story as the kids asked for a dragon to eat the car, or a giant chicken to crush a building. The easel was always a big hit.

"That's *your* thing," Ethan said. "I can't draw."

"That's not what Vika and her dad said." He ruffled Ethan's hair. "You can do it."

And before Ethan could object, he slipped out the front door.

Paralyzed, Ethan stared at the little kids and thought, *This is going to be a disaster.*

Sarah's birthday had already gotten off to a rocky start that morning when they'd given her her presents. Dad had saved the robotic dog for last. Ethan helped her unwrap it, and when she saw the picture on the box, she shouted excitedly, "Lucy!"

They unpacked the dog and switched it on. It was a pretty amazing toy, Ethan thought. The hair felt like real hair, and the way the eyes opened and closed was very lifelike. You could even feel a heartbeat if you put your hand firmly against the dog's chest. The dog wagged its tail. It panted. But Sarah stopped patting it within seconds.

"What's wrong?" Ethan asked.

"Sarah is disappointed," she said.

"Why?" Dad asked.

"This is not Lucy."

Ethan looked at Dad, who rolled his eyes.

"Well, even if it's not Lucy, she's still a lovely dog," Dad said, giving it an enthusiastic pat. "And it needs a name. What will you call it?"

But Sarah just asked if she could watch the new DVD Ethan had given her and retreated to the TV room.

Now, looking at Sarah running around with the other kids, Ethan took a deep breath, feeling angry at Dad. A few of the moms had offered to stay and help, but Dad had said, "No, no, everything's fine, don't worry about a thing!"

Mom would never have forgotten the cake. Ethan was startled by how much he missed her all of a sudden. She'd always run the parties. Dad was doing an okay job. He'd invited Sarah's friends, and he'd bought a piñata shaped like one of her favorite TV characters. He'd bought presents. But there were also things he'd forgotten, like the balloons tied to the back of the birthday girl's chair, and the shiny HAPPY BIRTHDAY banner taped above the kitchen doorway. Mom would've had a craft activity planned, and made sandwiches with the crusts cut off, and had a platter with vegetables.

Without Mom, the house still felt emptier, every room of it. Some mornings when Ethan woke up, he had that same terrible feeling he'd had right after she died. It made him want to curl himself up into a ball. Like if he made himself small enough, it wouldn't hurt so much.

"Okay, guys," he said, clapping his hands together, "who wants to draw!"

This worked. For about four minutes. Pretty soon kids were arguing over turns, fighting over the markers, or complaining someone was wrecking their picture. One of the girls was drawing all over her own face. Ethan gently pried the marker out of her hand.

"Can't *you* draw for us?" said Eva, who'd been to last year's party. She had a huge, infectious smile, but Ethan remembered that she was actually a bit of a demon.

"Yeah!" said two other kids.

They all sat down on the floor without being asked and looked up at him expectantly.

"So," said Ethan, "what do you guys want? How about a gorilla?"

"A giraffe!"

Ethan's heart sank. At the easel, he tried his best to do a giraffe.

One of the kids giggled. "That's not a giraffe!"

"Do a pony!"

His pony was even worse than his giraffe. He went through a few more animals.

"You're a bad drawer," said Eva.

"Where's Dada?" Sarah asked, noticing for the first time that Dad was missing. Ethan thought she looked a bit worried. He checked his watch. Only fifteen minutes had passed.

"Just give me one second," he said, and ran to his room.

He found Inkling underneath the bed.

"I need a favor," he said, and invited Inkling to slide onto his hand.

Back in the living room, Ethan stood beside the easel and said, "Guys, this is a very special easel."

"No it's not," said Eva. "I've got the same one at home."

"Yeah, it *is* special, and I'll tell you why. Because it's magic! Tell it what you want it to draw, and it'll do it!"

"An eagle!" a kid shouted.

From the bottom of the easel, a beautiful golden eagle soared up to fill the paper.

Everyone gasped. The eagle flapped its wings and soared right off the edge of the easel, disappearing.

"How'd you do that?" Eva demanded.

Ethan shrugged. "Magic, like I told you."

All at once, the kids started hollering out their requests.

• • •

The kids were so excited, and yelling so loudly, that Ethan almost didn't hear Dad coming in the front door.

Ethan stepped quickly to the easel and let Inkling slide off onto his hand.

"Thanks," he whispered.

Dad poked his head into the room and grinned. "Told you you'd be fine."

"You better take over," Ethan said.

Things went pretty smoothly after that. Dad drew for another fifteen minutes or so, while Ethan filled up the piñata. He overheard bratty Eva tell his dad that he wasn't as good as the magic easel. Afterward, he helped the kids whack the piñata until it burst open and all the treats spilled to the floor.

Dad hadn't prepared much in the way of food, but the kids seemed happy enough with the bowls of cheese puffs and potato chips while they watched a DVD. Ethan thought this was a pretty lame birthday activity, since most of the kids had probably seen the movie already. But Sarah was also simultaneously opening her presents and didn't mind that her guests were playing with them, too.

"It's time for the cake now," Ethan reminded his dad after a while. "Their parents are coming soon."

"Right, yeah," said Dad. "Okay, will you get them to the table?"

It took a while to herd them to the dining room and into their chairs.

"Vanilla cake with chocolate icing!" Sarah cried out with huge enthusiasm.

Ethan went to the kitchen to make sure Dad remembered to put the candles on.

Dad was standing in front of the open fridge, frowning.

"What?" Ethan asked.

"Did you take the cake out of the fridge?"

"I haven't touched it," Ethan said. "I haven't even seen it."

Dad turned in a slow circle, his eyes darting round the kitchen.

"I paid for it," he said, "and then . . . I must've left it on the counter!"

"You forgot the cake again?"

"No, I just . . . forgot to carry it out!"

"The kids are getting picked up in ten minutes!"

"Cake!" someone screamed from the dining room.

"There's no time to go pick it up," Dad said. "We can improvise."

"How do you improvise a cake?"

From the fridge, Dad grabbed a loaf of sliced bread and slapped it onto the counter.

"No," said Ethan.

Dad slipped it out of the bag, then rummaged in some drawers, found an elastic band, and stretched it around the entire loaf to keep it together. The ends got a bit squished.

"Oh yeah," said Dad. "They won't even notice. We'll call this"—he snatched a jar of Nutella from the cupboard—"vanilla loaf cake."

"Wait, wait!" said Ethan. "That's hazelnut! There might be allergies!"

Dad looked exasperated. "Well, just go ask them!"

"They're little kids! They might not know!"

"Fine!" Dad rummaged around in the cupboard above the fridge where Mom had kept all the baking supplies. "Yes!"

He pulled down a dented tin of chocolate icing and peeled back the lid. Ethan leaned in for a look and winced.

"We can just . . . add a bit of hot water and loosen it up a bit," Dad mumbled. "Can you get something to spread it with?"

When they were done, it was the ugliest cake Ethan had ever seen, but at least it held eight candles (and a ninth, which Ethan jammed in because Dad had forgotten how old Sarah was).

"Hang on," Ethan said. "What about the elastic band?"

His father faltered a moment. "It's good, it's good. Come on."

They marched into the dining room, singing "Happy Birthday" louder than they ever had before.

Sarah blew out the candles and then looked carefully at the cake but said nothing. Ethan thought it was best to serve it fast. With the first slice, he cut through the elastic band, and with a snap it whizzed across the table and hit the jug of cranberry juice, leaving a chocolaty smear.

"What happened?" Eva asked.

"Nothing," said Dad. He looked at Ethan. "Keep slicing."

It was very easy to slice. Within seconds, Dad had a piece in front of every kid at the table. As they chewed, all the kids had slightly puzzled expressions on their faces. For a few moments everyone was silent.

Then one of the girls from Sarah's playgroup said, "This is bread."

Ethan couldn't bring himself to lie to her, so he said nothing, just refilled everyone's glasses with juice.

"It's a loaf cake," said Dad, shoveling another forkful into his mouth. "Hmm! It tastes a little bit like bread, doesn't it?"

Luckily the doorbell rang, and the first parents arrived for pickup. Forks hit the plates as the kids fled the table.

As Ethan handed out the loot bags near the door, he saw one mother glance at the hideous remnants of the cake on the dining room table.

"What's that?" she asked her daughter quietly.

"That's the cake!" piped the girl. "It was *bread*!"

• • •

That night, Inkling returned to Mr. Rylance's bedroom and this time slid right up onto the pillow. Ethan's father was snoring again. His breath smelled like the empty glass of wine on his bedside table.

Inkling moved closer still. He was still scared of him, but he also somehow felt responsible for him.

Was Mr. Rylance dreaming? Inkling wanted to see the strange bed again—he wanted to see all of it this time, without Rickman interrupting. Would Ethan's dad even *have* the same dream again?

Right away, Inkling was drawing on the white pillow. He had no control over it. It was all automatic, just flowing through him. A piñata being whacked with a stick. A cake that someone was reaching for but just kept getting farther and farther away.

It wasn't long, though, before Inkling found himself sketching the high bed again. The railings, the wheels, the ridges in the ugly green blanket, and then the person in the bed.

As Inkling drew, it wasn't just a picture he was creating, it was a whole storm of feelings from Mr. Rylance's sleeping mind. Loneliness and sadness and anger and regret. It was almost too much to bear, but Inkling finished the picture, erased it, and fled.

Back in Ethan's bedroom, Inkling found the piece of paper on which he'd started the picture of the terrible bed—and now completed it.

• • •

Ethan was woken by his sister climbing over his back.

"Sarah, it's only— Ow! That really hurt!" He pushed her poky elbow off his neck.

"Can she have a cuddle?" Sarah asked, scrabbling across his body and thrashing her way under the sheets.

The clock said 6:37. Sarah was a notoriously early riser.

"Yeah," Ethan said grumpily, "but don't poke me anymore. And I want to sleep, okay?"

He sank down lower under the blanket. He usually didn't mind having her in bed with him, but she was a wriggler, and a talker. This time, though, she was on her best behavior. All he was aware of was the warmth of her small body as he drifted back off to sleep.

When he woke, Sarah was gone and he could hear the sound of one of her shows from the TV room. He leaned over and peeked underneath his bed.

"Inkling?"

When Inkling didn't appear, he went to check the comic drawer, but it was empty. From the corner of his eye, he caught a smudge of movement from the bookshelf, and saw Inkling emerge from a book called *The Old Man and the Sea* by Ernest Hemingway. Ethan remembered it was about an old man who catches the biggest fish in the world.

"Did you finish it?" Ethan asked.

YES.

"I liked that one."

IT WAS GOOD.

"The part when the sharks come, that was really exciting."

THE WRITING WAS GOOD AND CLEAN AND TRUE. IT WAS GOOD TO READ IT. IT WAS GOOD TO READ ONE CLEAN, TRUE SENTENCE AFTER THE OTHER.

"Um, yeah," said Ethan. Was that the way people talked in the book?

I LIKED THE GOOD, PLAIN LANGUAGE. I HAVE BEEN USING TOO MANY WORDS. I WILL USE FEWER.

"Just because the book talks that way doesn't mean you have to," Ethan said.

NO. I AM DECIDED.

"Okay. Can we work on the project after breakfast?"

YES.

Ethan didn't smell coffee or any other breakfast smells as

he walked to the kitchen. There was no sign of his father. He checked the TV room. Sarah was standing in front of the TV, wiggling her fingers.

"Hey, Sarah, where's Dad?"

On weekends, usually Dad made her breakfast and let her eat it in front of the TV.

"In the big bed."

It was weird for Dad not to be up. Ethan went and quietly poked his head into the room.

"Dad?"

He heard a grunt.

"You getting up?"

"In a bit. Can you do breakfast?"

Ethan grimaced. "Um, yeah, okay."

At least it was a Sunday, so he didn't have to worry about picking out Sarah's clothes for school. He got her a bowl of Cheerios, made scrambled eggs (Mom had taught him a while ago), and put some on a plate for Sarah with a big splotch of ketchup. She wanted ketchup with pretty much everything.

He ate his own breakfast with her, sitting cross-legged on the sofa. Occasionally she'd come over and throw an arm around him, then go back to the TV. Afterward, she wanted to play animal checkup, and then indoor catch with one of her soft toys. After that, Ethan was bored and grumpy. He wanted to get to work on his graphic novel. He swung by Dad's room again.

"Dad? It's ten-thirty."

Dad was turned away so Ethan couldn't see his face, but Ethan had the feeling he wasn't asleep. He just wasn't answering.

Ethan closed the door behind him, loudly. First Dad left him alone at the birthday party, and now he wouldn't even get out of bed! Ethan let Sarah watch more TV. Why should he play with her all day?

At around eleven there was a knock on the door, and Ethan opened it to Soren standing astride his bike.

"Want to go ride in the park?"

"Yeah, but I can't. I've got to watch Sarah."

"Where's your dad?"

"Sleeping."

Soren nodded. "I can hang out here for a bit."

Ethan was glad to see him. They hadn't talked much since Soren had asked to use Inkling for his history test and Ethan had basically said no. He didn't want to confess how he didn't want to share Inkling with anyone.

"Inkling's teaching me how to draw," he told Soren after he came inside. "So I'm going to start doing the drawings myself. Want to see?"

From his bedroom, he got the illustration board and markers—and Inkling—and in the kitchen he showed Soren how they worked together.

"I'm still pretty slow," Ethan said.

YOU WILL IMPROVE, Inkling wrote. **WE WILL WORK EVERY DAY.**

"Thanks, Inkling."

YOU MUST HAVE COURAGE. IF YOU DRAW ONE TRUE
LINE AFTER ANOTHER, YOU WILL NOT FAIL.

"Who's he talking like now?" Soren asked.

"I think he's still on Ernest Hemingway."

"Well," said Soren, "looks like you've got yourself the best teacher possible."

"It's still kind of cheating, but it's not as bad as before."

"I get it," said Soren. "I'm memorizing dates for the history test, by the way."

It was past lunchtime now, so Ethan heated up some soup and made grilled cheese sandwiches for everyone. He cut Sarah's into triangles because she liked dipping them into the soup.

Afterward, Soren had to take off for home. When Ethan looked in on Sarah, she smelled a bit poopy, but he didn't want to check whether she'd had an accident. That was Dad's job.

Ethan paced the living room. Now that Soren had left, he felt a lot lonelier. Worse, he was starting to feel scared. It was almost three o'clock, and Dad was still in bed. Was he having some kind of nervous breakdown? What if he never got up? After Mom died, there'd been a few times Dad stayed in bed all day. Ethan had a terrifying image of Dad being taken away to the hospital in an ambulance. What would happen to him and Sarah?

He went into the dark bedroom. "Dad, you've got to get up!"

"Yep." He didn't move.

The room was stuffy and unpleasant. Ethan yanked up the blinds and opened a window. He felt a bit less afraid with fresh air and sunlight pouring in. He dragged the blankets off Dad. Dad slept in boxers and a T-shirt. He looked surprisingly pale and somehow smaller than normal. For a second Ethan felt sorry for him.

"Okay!" Dad said, slowly sitting. "Thank you."

"I think Sarah needs a change," Ethan said.

"I'm on it."

Ethan kicked at the carpet. "I looked after her all day!"

Dad's shoulders lifted and fell heavily. "I'm sorry."

Ethan didn't know whether to slam the door or hug his dad. In the end, he just walked out.

CHAPTER 10

"**D**ad is such an idiot," Ethan said to Inkling.

With a sigh, he lifted his marker off the illustration board. He couldn't concentrate on his drawing. Suddenly he was telling Inkling everything—how worried he was about Dad, and how angry. How tired he was of always being the one to play with Sarah. He even talked about how things were so much better when Mom was alive, and how much he missed her.

Inkling was still for a moment, as if mulling things over. Then he wrote:

HE HAS SAD DREAMS.

"How do you know that?"

I SEE THEM.

"You can't see people's dreams!" But even as Ethan said it, he thought, *Why not?* Inkling was like some piece of Dad come loose. A bit of his imagination running around all over the place, like a stray dog.

I ONLY SEE HIS DREAMS, NOT ANYONE ELSE'S. I DREW A PICTURE.

Inkling darted underneath the bed. Ethan got down on his belly and peered into the mess of newspapers and ancient, forgotten stuff.

"Inkling?"

A long, inky line slithered out to him. He followed it with his hand, sifting through papers until he saw Inkling making a thumbs-up sign on a particular piece of newsprint. He pulled it out. It was blank on one side, but when he turned it over, he saw a picture of a woman in a hospital room. He could tell it was a hospital room by all the equipment on the walls and the railings around the bed. But it took him a few seconds to recognize the woman.

"Is that Mom?" he asked softly.

YES.

Ethan felt like a fist had clenched inside his chest. Mom's face was puffy. Her long, curly hair was limp. There were tubes in her nostrils and taped to her arms.

He'd never seen her like this. When she got really sick, Dad said she hadn't wanted him or Sarah to visit the hospital. She didn't look like herself, Dad explained. She didn't want him and Sarah to be upset. Maybe when she felt a little better. But there hadn't been a better. Ethan had never had a chance to say good-bye to her.

Furious, he crumpled up the paper with Inkling inside and hurled it across the room. He didn't want to remember Mom like this. She didn't look the way she was supposed to. She looked sick and ugly.

From the crumpled paper, Inkling emerged and glided across the floor toward him.

"Why'd you show me this?"

THIS IS WHAT HE DREAMS.

"Big deal! Of course he misses her! We all miss her. But he's just got to . . . get over it! He's a grown-up. He can't just stay in bed all day!"

HE IS STUCK.

"Well, he better get unstuck!" muttered Ethan.

THERE IS SOMETHING HE NEEDS.

"Yeah. Mom back, but that's impossible." He sighed. "What he needs is to get unblocked."

UNBLOCKED?

"Yeah, he can't come up with a new story. I looked in his sketchbook yesterday and he hasn't done anything since . . ." He hadn't realized it until now. "Since you jumped out."

On the floor, Inkling seemed to shrivel up a bit.

"No, no, it's not like it's your fault," Ethan said. "He was blocked way before you came. But it's like you're definitely part of him. He made you with his ink, with his inspiration, and . . ."

He thought for a moment.

"Do you think you could help him?"

THERE IS SOMETHING— Inkling began to write, but Ethan interrupted.

"Do you think you could draw a new graphic novel for him?"

Inkling seemed to consider this.

LIKE WHAT WE'RE DOING?

"Sort of, yeah!"

WHAT IS THE STORY?

Ethan hadn't thought this far ahead. "Well, I don't know. Can't you just make one up?"

Inkling swayed back and forth thoughtfully.

CAN IT BE THE STORY, TOLD WELL AND TRULY, OF A MAN WHO CATCHES A GREAT FISH?

"Well, no, that would be too much like *The Old Man and the Sea*."

OR THE STORY OF AN ORPHANED GIRL WHO GOES TO LIVE ON A FARM ON PRINCE EDWARD ISLAND?

"No—"

OR THE TALE OF A GIRL SNATCHED BY A GIANT—

"Inkling! It has to be an original story!"

I CAN'T DO IT.

Ethan blinked in surprise. "Why not?"

I JUST DRAW. I NEED A STORY.

Ethan thought about this. It was true. They'd *given* Inkling the story of the gorilla. He'd read Soren's script, then used Ethan's stick figures as a guide to make the drawings.

"Well," he said, "how about if we feed you more books? As many as you like! Especially Dad's, all the best ones, just so you get a sense of the way he writes—I mean, maybe you know that already. Would that be enough? And then you could just sort of mix them all together. Sort of like Sarah does when she makes up her own stories."

I WILL TRY. I MIGHT FAIL. BUT A MAN WHO DOES NOT TRY CAN NEVER TRULY BE A MAN.

Ethan figured Inkling would stop talking like Ernest Hemingway as soon as he read some other stories.

"And look," he said. "I'm not asking you to do the whole thing. Maybe just start Dad off with one big double-page spread, and that'll be enough to unblock him!"

YES.

"Come on, let's have a look." He put out his hand and Inkling flowed onto it, giving him that cool, fluttery feeling. It was like a spring breeze. It was like something waiting to happen.

In the hallway, Ethan paused and listened to make sure his father was still in the kitchen. He smelled coffee and felt comforted.

When he crossed the threshold of Dad's studio, his wrist suddenly pricked with gooseflesh. He looked down and saw Inkling trembling.

"What's wrong?"

THIS ROOM FRIGHTENS ME, Inkling wrote on his arm.

"Why?"

I FEAR THE SKETCHBOOK.

Ethan frowned, then remembered how he'd once threatened to put Inkling back inside.

"Oh, I was just kidding, Inkling! It's only a book. Paper. You love paper!"

Inkling stopped shaking.

YES. A MAN MUST FACE FEAR. THAT IS WHAT A MAN DOES.

There were several bookcases in his father's studio. The one closest to his drafting table was where he kept his favorite books. Plenty were ones that Ethan had read and loved, too: graphic novels and comics, science fiction epics and historical adventure stories.

He made a small pile on Dad's drafting table and opened the cover of the first book, *Twenty Thousand Leagues Under the Sea*.

"Dad always said this was a really good one. Maybe we should star—"

Inkling slid right onto the title page, eagerly slurping up the title, the author's name, the illustration, and all the little, boring bits at the bottom.

"I didn't mean right now," Ethan whispered, looking over his shoulder nervously.

Impatiently, Inkling poured himself between the pages and disappeared. It suddenly occurred to Ethan that his plan involved completely erasing Dad's favorite books.

Some of them were really nice hardbacks. He sighed. He'd worry about it later. Maybe he could buy new ones with his allowance.

He was about to lift the pile of books back to his room when he saw Dad's sketchbook on the far side of the table. He'd checked it yesterday morning, and he knew he wouldn't find any new sketches now, but he couldn't help himself. He opened it up and turned through the pages. The sketches stopped at the same place as last time.

From the corner of his eye, he saw *Twenty Thousand Leagues Under the Sea* bleeding ink. He frowned. A thin black ribbon oozed down the stack of books onto the drafting table.

"Inkling?" he whispered. "What're you doing?"

Inkling was snaking very slowly across the table. He twitched and started to write while in motion, but the letters just got smeared before he could finish a word.

From outside the studio, Ethan heard his father coming down the hallway.

"Inkling," he whispered, "come on, we've got to go!"

He laid his hand on the table, but Inkling just flowed right over it—heading in the direction of Dad's open sketchbook.

"No!" Ethan gasped, suddenly understanding.

The sketchbook was *dragging* Inkling toward it. It had dragged Inkling right out of the novel, and Inkling was fighting against the pull but losing. Ethan tried to grab hold of him, digging in with his fingers. Inkling seeped right through, flowing faster now. When Inkling touched the binding of the sketchbook, he jerked back as if burned.

"Ethan, you in there?" Dad called out, steps away from the door.

Ethan slammed the sketchbook shut. At that exact moment, Inkling gave a great shudder and pulled himself clear.

Ethan turned to face his father as he walked in.

"Just looking for something to read," he said, picking up *Twenty Thousand Leagues Under the Sea.* He caught a flash of Inkling disappearing amongst the pages. "Mind if I borrow this?"

"Be my guest. It's a good one. Hey, sorry I slept so late. That party kind of took it out of me."

His dad really did look apologetic.

"It wasn't so bad," Ethan lied.

He felt like Dad wanted to say something more, but Ethan was worried about Inkling and wanted to check on him. So he grabbed the pile of books and hurried back to his room. Inside the novel, Inkling slowly rocked himself back and forth on a half-eaten page.

"Are you okay? What happened?"

THE SKETCHBOOK WANTS ME BACK.

"I don't get it! No other books do that to you!"

IT'S THE PAPER I CAME FROM.

Ethan nodded. He felt so stupid. In their first meeting, Inkling had even shown him how hard it was to pull free of the book. There was a good reason he'd been so scared when they entered the studio.

"What would happen?" he asked. "If it sucked you in."

I WOULD BE FIXED. NOTHING MORE THAN INK.

"I'm really sorry, Inkling. I should've known. It won't happen again, I promise."

• • •

During dinner, while Ethan ate, Inkling was eating, too. And late into the evening, he ate some more, soaring through all the books and graphic novels Ethan had picked out for him.

By bedtime Inkling was positively trembling with all these new stories. It was like he'd had too much coffee and couldn't sit still. Even as he read, little bits of him kept flashing out to sketch the people and things he was reading about.

"I think you've probably had enough now," Ethan said as Inkling finished the last title in the Kren series. He was worried Inkling would explode if he read any more.

Inkling sloshed about on the blank endpapers, twitching, scribbling little words to himself, then erasing them.

"You okay?" Ethan asked.

THE WORLD IS TRULY FILLED WITH WONDROUS STORIES.

"Do you think you can come up with one?"

I WILL DO MY UTMOST.

It was hard to know what voice Inkling was speaking in at the moment. Ethan supposed it was a big, bubbling mix of all the books he'd just absorbed.

"I'm sure whatever you come up with will be great."

Ethan got a fresh piece of illustration board and slid it under the bed.

CAN I MAKE USE OF COLOR?

"Yeah. Of course. The more the better!"

TREMENDOUS! I ADORE COLOR!

"Do you need light under there?"

I'M FINE.

Ethan turned off the lights but couldn't sleep. Underneath his bed a magical creature was drawing something incredible. He listened but heard nothing. He couldn't remember if Inkling made noise when he drew. There was certainly no swish or squeak of a brush or marker. After a few more minutes, he turned on his lamp and leaned down to look under his bed.

Inkling was just resting on the board. He hadn't made a single jot yet.

"What's wrong?"

NOT A THING. I'M PONDERING.

"Oh, okay."

IT'S NO EASY THING, CREATING A STORY.

"Sure. Take your time. Well, not too much time. Dad's got to snap out of this or we'll all go down the drain."

PLEASE BE QUIET.

"Okay. Good night."

He tried to sleep but started worrying that Inkling wouldn't be able to do it. He'd asked too much. He'd asked Inkling to do something overnight that his father hadn't been able to do in two years!

But eventually, Ethan fell asleep.

• • •

And at some point in the night, Inkling trembled and moved to the top-left corner of the illustration board. A few tendrils reached out, flexed like they were limbering up—

And then began to draw.

• • •

That same night, across the neighborhood, Vika was woken by the sound of her mom and dad talking in their bedroom. They weren't arguing, exactly, but her mom sounded upset. Vika sat up, listening.

". . . really that serious?" her mom was saying.

Vika missed the first bit of what her dad said, but heard, ". . . last two years, sales have been really bad. We're in debt."

"But the house?" her mom said. "Is it that bad?"

Fear jolted through Vika. What about the house? She moved closer to the door so she could hear better.

"No, no," her dad said. "We're fine for now. I'm talking in a year or two."

"What about Peter's new project?"

"Yeah, if he ever finishes it!" her dad said. "And it would have to be a huge bestseller. Sometimes I worry he might be . . ."

Vika didn't catch the next bit and pressed her ear hard against the door.

"He wouldn't do something like that," her mom said.

"Who knows? He hasn't shown me anything for so long."

"It's been a very tough time for him."

"It has, for sure. But for all I know, he's working on something for another publisher. Marvel's been after him for a while. . . ."

Vika couldn't stand still; she paced her room. Hearing her

dad sound all stressed made her scared—and then it made her angry. Why was Peter Rylance just sitting around doing nothing when her dad needed a bestseller to save his company? Or was Mr. Rylance working on something for another publisher? Stabbing her dad in the back?

She tornado-kicked the air a few times. Peter Rylance wouldn't even *be* famous if it weren't for her father. He was the one who published his first Kren book after everyone else had rejected it.

When she got older, she'd make her own graphic novels, and her dad wouldn't have to rely on Peter Rylance or any of those other wimpy artists who couldn't write bestsellers. Or who missed their deadlines. Or who got blocked. Vika never missed her deadlines.

And there was definitely something weird going on in the Rylance house.

She hadn't told her dad, or anyone, about what she'd seen in Ethan's room that night. She was almost a hundred percent sure it wasn't her imagination, no matter what Ethan said.

She didn't know what Ethan and his dad were doing.

But she was going to find out.

CHAPTER 11

When Ethan woke up, he was almost afraid to look underneath his bed. He lay still for a few moments, hoping, and then reached down. His fingers touched the board, and he pulled it out.

He sucked in his breath. It was an entire world he held in his hands. The colors blazed. His gaze was swept along through one beautiful image after another. It was wordless, but he felt like an amazing story was about to begin. It looked so much like his father's work it was uncanny.

"Inkling," he said. "Inkling?"

He jumped out of bed and crouched down. When he saw Inkling huddled on a pile of newsprint, he gave a small cry of surprise. Inkling was a dingy gray color, as if he'd been diluted by dirty water. It looked like he was shivering.

"Inkling, what's wrong?"

JUST A BIT FATIGUED.

"Was it too much work? I'm sorry, Inkling. Let me get you some real food!"

He hurried around his room, dragging out the last few uneaten comics from his drawer. Inkling needed color and energy. From his bookshelf, Ethan also grabbed some books. He opened them all in front of Inkling, inviting him to eat. Sluggishly, Inkling moved onto the nearest comic. Like an ancient cat, he lapped out a pale tongue and lifted the ink off the page. Then took another lick. A few more licks, and then he was still. He didn't look quite so pale now.

THANKS, ETHAN.

"Inkling, this work is amazing! You've done a fantastic job."

Wearily Inkling formed himself into a smiley face.

"Thank you so much."

At school that day, Ethan worried. Mostly, about Inkling. He'd seemed so exhausted. Before this, all he'd been doing was black-and-white drawings for Ethan's graphic novel, but what he created last night was on a whole other scale. The colors, the sweep of it—and the beginnings of a story that somehow Inkling had created all by himself. That was something he'd never done before! No wonder he was wiped out.

Ethan was also worried about his father. Would he be pleased when he saw Inkling's work after school?

He just hoped it would smash through Dad's castle-sized block.

• • •

After school, Dad stared at the double-page spread on Ethan's desk, a deep furrow across his forehead. Nervously, Ethan watched and waited.

"Is this yours?" Dad finally asked him.

"No."

He puffed out air. "Well, it's someone doing a heck of a good imitation of me. Who did it?"

"Well, you, really."

"No, I'd remember doing this. It's not mine. Where'd you get this, Ethan?"

"You have to promise to listen, and let me finish."

His father sat down in the chair, and Ethan told him everything. With every sentence he knew it sounded more and more like something from a comic book, but what was he supposed to do? It was the truth. When he finished, his father said nothing, gently swiveling to and fro in the chair, staring at the artwork. When he finally looked at his son, there was real concern in his eyes.

"Ethan, I know things haven't been easy—"

"Dad, I'm not crazy!"

"I never said you were! But I'm wondering if there might be another explanation for—"

"Why don't you just meet him?"

"Inkling?" Dad looked more concerned than ever and was a bit lost for words. "Okay, sure." He was talking more slowly and softly than usual, like a therapist from a movie. "Do you want to describe him to me?"

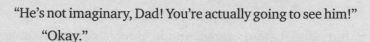

"He's not imaginary, Dad! You're actually going to see him!"

"Okay."

"He's like a big splotch of ink."

"Got it."

Ethan sighed and turned to his bed. "Inkling, come meet my dad."

Underneath the bed, Inkling had been listening. He wanted to make a good impression on Mr. Rylance. He wanted to be likable. Puppies were likable, and the only thing better than a puppy was a really, really *huge* puppy.

He came bounding out, tongue lolling, the size of a rabid timber wolf.

"Holy *crap*!" Ethan's dad shouted, pushing back in the chair so hard that it fell over with him in it. "Ethan, get out of here! It's a freakin' monster!"

He grabbed his son's hockey stick and started whacking Inkling.

"Dad! Stop!"

The giant puppy pranced around playfully, easily avoiding the hockey stick.

"Inkling!" Ethan shouted. "Just be small, okay?"

Instantly, Inkling shrank and slid onto Ethan's outstretched hand.

Dad sat panting on the floor. "What the heck *is* that?"

"It's Inkling, just like I've been telling you!"

Slowly Mr. Rylance stood and watched Ethan carry Inkling to the desk. He glided off onto a piece of blank paper and wrote:

HELLO, MR. RYLANCE. I'M SORRY I FRIGHTENED YOU.

Ethan watched his father's Adam's apple bob up and down. Then Dad paced the room, his hands clasped over the top his head, taking big, noisy breaths in and out, and muttering to himself. He kept taking quick little glances over at Inkling, then looking away and shaking his head some more.

"Dad?" Ethan said. "Dad!"

"Yeah," his father said.

"It's real."

"Yeah, okay." He stopped pacing, came closer. "So. He came from my sketchbook?"

"Yes."

"And he's been helping you draw?"

Ethan had already told him all this, but it was like Dad needed to ask a few questions that he already knew the answers to. Ethan nodded. Dad warily approached the desk and looked down at Inkling, who was gently expanding and contracting like a jellyfish.

"What do I do?" Dad asked Ethan.

"Maybe say hello."

"Hello, Inkling," he said weakly, then added, "Sorry about the hockey stick. The dog was just very . . . realistic."

HE WAS PERHAPS A BIT LARGE.

Dad nodded. He scratched his head. "Can I see you draw?"

CERTAINLY. WHAT WOULD YOU LIKE ME TO DRAW?

"Anything's good."

Inkling hesitated a moment and then began a picture of a suited man sitting in a diner at night. Light poured through the windows out onto a city street. Ethan watched his father's intent face.

"Stop, please," Dad said before the drawing was complete.

"What's wrong?" Ethan asked.

His father righted the chair and sat down in it. "Nothing. It's amazing. It's just so . . . strange. It's like watching myself draw, only I'm not doing it."

"He's a part of you, jumped free from the sketchbook."

"Yeah," Dad murmured. His eyes went back to the glorious double-page spread Inkling had created during the night. "And this . . ."

"Do you like it?" Ethan asked anxiously.

Dad looked at him solemnly. "You asked him to do this for me?"

"Well, I just thought it might help . . ."

"Get me unblocked?"

"Maybe just get your imagination going, yeah."

His dad came over and gave him a hug. "Thank you. You don't have to worry about me, you know. Everything's okay."

Ethan nodded, but he wasn't so sure. He didn't think it was okay to not work for so long or to stay in bed all day. But it felt good to be hugged. It felt good to see Dad grin and to be told things were all right.

"What do you think of it, though?" Ethan asked again, nodding at the spread.

"I think," Dad said, "that it's fantastic."

• • •

Dad took them out to their favorite Italian restaurant.

"Pasketti!" shouted Sarah before they were even seated. "With Parmesan!"

They got one of the cozy booths. The restaurant was always bustling, and there were old Italian street signs and posters on the walls, and shelves with colorful jars of tomatoes and peppers and olives. Light danced off the zinc bar, behind which was a huge, ancient coffee machine that sounded like a steam engine.

While they waited for their meals, Sarah was full of stories about Lucy, her puppy—and not even Dad seemed to mind tonight. Ethan ordered a Limonata, and Sarah had milk with a straw, and Dad had a pale red wine, and they talked about Inkling, in between listening to Sarah.

"He stays under your bed the whole time?" Dad asked.

"Mostly. I keep newspapers for him to eat. He likes comics a lot, but they make him hyper. I've been trying to give him more books."

It was such a relief for Ethan to finally tell his father. A secret was a heavy thing to carry around for so long, and day by day it only got heavier. He realized that this was the most he and his dad had talked about *anything* in a long time.

"He reads a lot at night. I think he wanders around, too," Ethan added, but he couldn't bring himself to mention how Inkling had drawn Dad's dreams. It was too personal. "Oh, and he's terrified of Rickman for some reason."

"Rickman?" Dad said, laughing.

"Icklan is a naughty cat!" Sarah interjected.

"A terribly naughty cat!" Dad agreed, which pleased Sarah no end.

He took another sip of his wine and shook his head thoughtfully. "That spread Inkling did. It was like something I might've dreamed. The colors. And the energy across the page. There's a setting and a character and something about to happen."

"So you think you'll be able to use it?" Ethan asked hopefully.

His father rocked his head side to side. "Well, it's certainly not the same direction I'd been leaning toward. . . ."

Ethan tried to hide his disappointment, but his father must've seen, because he said, "It's amazing, don't get me wrong. I feel like the door to a new world has just been kicked open."

"Yeah," said Ethan. "I mean, just looking at it, don't you have a million ideas of what might happen next?"

"It's very intriguing. I'll need to look at it some more.

Shouldn't we keep him somewhere safer?"

"Inkling?" Ethan blinked. "Like where?"

"Someplace Rickman can't get him."

"Well, Rickman can't really hurt him—"

"And where he can't escape."

Ethan was startled by the choice of word. *Escape* meant wanting to get away from something terrible.

"I don't think he wants to go anywhere," Ethan said, but he suddenly remembered how Inkling had wandered off into the art room. That was just curiosity, though. He'd smelled ink. He'd been hoping to find other creatures like himself. Would he try again?

Ethan realized how much he wanted Inkling to stay, and not just because he needed his help. Inkling was like a friend now. Surely if he'd wanted to escape, he would have done it by now. All he had to do was slip under the door, and he could go anywhere.

"To Inkling, then," Dad said, raising his glass.

Ethan clinked with him, and Sarah insisted on clinking her milk glass, too, and Ethan thought that things were definitely looking up.

• • •

Next morning, as he woke up, Ethan smelled coffee and bacon. He lay in bed for a few more minutes, smiling, just listening to the comforting kitchen sounds: cutlery clinking, fridge door closing, toaster popping, the muted sounds of Dad talking to Sarah.

When he went to the kitchen, Dad was already dressed, and he'd gotten Sarah dressed and was making her scrambled eggs. He had lots of coffee in him and was now Alert Dad.

"Hey, sleepyhead," Dad greeted him.

"You're up early."

"Time to get serious about work," Alert Dad said.

He certainly looked and sounded energetic, and Ethan grinned. He could remember the times when Dad's work was going well. Maybe he'd meet his four-month deadline after all.

"You've got an idea?" Ethan asked hopefully.

"Let's just say I feel something ready to bang on the door."

• • •

When Ethan got home from school, he found Dad in his studio, asleep on the little sofa.

"Hey," Ethan said worriedly. "How's it going?"

"Oh, good. Good! Just taking a little nap!"

Ethan wondered if there was an exclamation-mark lie in there somewhere. Dad must have seen the uncertainty in his face, because he said, "Want to see?"

He got up, stretched, and walked to the drafting table.

"Oh, wow!" said Ethan.

It was a glorious full page: inked, colored, lettered. And it was definitely a continuation of Inkling's double-page spread. Ethan recognized the main character and the landscape.

"Dad, this is amazing!"

"It turned out pretty well, huh?"

"I can't believe you did this all in one day!" He looked around the drafting table. Usually after Dad finished a page, there'd be pencil cartoons and roughs and color tests scattered all over the place. The table was surprisingly tidy, and Dad was not a tidy person.

"I had a little help," Dad admitted.

Ethan looked at him. "What d'you mean?"

"I spent a long time looking at that opening spread, and it was incredible. You could stare at it for hours. Beautiful. But really, it was just a mood piece. There's a girl looking over the jungle, and there's a village and maybe, way off, a tomb. It feels like an adventure, like *something* about to begin. But what? And is it on earth, or another world? Those creatures up in the sky, are they normal birds? So many questions. I just thought Inkling might have some of the answers."

"So you asked him what happened next?" Ethan said.

Dad shrugged. "Why not? He came up with the opening image, so maybe he'd already imagined a bit of the rest."

"I thought you were just . . . you know, going to do your own thing with it," Ethan said.

"Sure, but what was the point of me making it up if Inkling already *knew*? And he did. He even offered to sketch out the next little bit for me."

Ethan's eyes widened. "You brought him in here? I told you about the sketchbook!"

"Don't worry, I kept it closed and moved it way out of the way."

Ethan felt the same stab he'd had when Soren asked to borrow Inkling. "So he just roughed in a few panels for you?"

At this Dad looked sheepish. "Bit more than that."

"Coloring?"

"Some coloring, yes."

"The dialogue?"

"He came up with some very good lines."

Ethan was surprised how indignant he felt. He really didn't like the idea of Inkling working with his dad. A day ago, all he'd hoped for was his father getting back to work. But now he couldn't stop himself saying, "So he's basically doing everything?"

"He's just giving me a good push," Dad replied.

It seemed to Ethan like this was already more than a push, but he didn't say anything.

"I doubt I'll need him anymore after today," Dad added. "And anyway, he's part of my imagination, right? These are my ideas."

"I guess." Ethan supposed he had a point, but it didn't feel quite true. It was hard to think of Inkling as being part of Dad, when he seemed so much his own . . . *person*. Still, Dad was so cheerful now, and it was such a relief to see a new piece of work on his drafting table.

Ethan went to his room to find Inkling. All day, he'd been looking forward to his drawing lesson, to seeing his own graphic novel grow panel by panel. It was his favorite time of day, just the two of them, working quietly together. Inkling was a patient teacher—and Ethan knew Dad wouldn't be nearly as patient, or as encouraging.

For the first time in a long time, things felt good again.

CHAPTER 12

At lunchtime the next day, Vika signed herself out of school and rode her bike to the Rylances' house. She cycled past it to the end of the block, locked her bike to a pole, then went back on foot.

The car was in the driveway, so she knew Mr. Rylance was home—no surprise, since his studio was in the house. She knew she'd have to be really careful. Quickly she walked down the side of the house, through the tall, ratty grass.

Every time she passed a window, she ducked. When she got to Ethan's room, she stopped and peeped inside. She grimaced. The blinds were still angled closed. She pressed her face against the glass and tried to peek through the cracks, but the lights were off inside, and she couldn't see anything.

She continued to the backyard. She remembered there used to be a nice garden, but it didn't look like anyone had taken care of it in a while. All the plots were overgrown, the plants strangled with weeds.

Mr. Rylance's studio had big windows and French doors overlooking the garden. Crouched down below one of the windows, Vika listened, then slowly lifted her head. She'd always admired the studio, the few times she'd been invited to see it. It was the kind of space she dreamed she herself might have one day. Off to the right was Mr. Rylance, head bent intently over his drafting table. He sat back for a moment, and Vika noticed there was no marker in his hand, yet something seemed to move on the illustration board. She frowned. Quickly, she moved over a few more windows to get a better view of the drafting table.

Across the paper slowly swirled an inky shadow, like a satellite image of a hurricane, only black. Its outer arms were busy making lines and brushstrokes, creating a beautiful colored picture of a girl running through a jungle.

Mr. Rylance said something, and the shadow hesitated, then reached back and added a bit more color and shading to the drawing, and also adjusted the angle of the girl's arm. Mr. Rylance nodded.

Vika suddenly realized she hadn't taken a breath in a long time. She ducked down and sucked in air as quietly as she could. Her heart pounded.

It was real.

Whatever she'd seen that night in Ethan's room, it was a real thing and it *drew*!

When she peeped up again, Mr. Rylance was putting the artwork facedown on a flatbed scanner and closing the cover. A bar of light started moving underneath. Mr. Rylance stood, stretched, and walked across the room toward the door. Vika flinched, afraid of being seen, but he wasn't even looking in her direction. Probably taking a bathroom break.

The ink splotch ambled across the drafting table now, twirling itself into interesting patterns while moving closer to some colorful pages ripped from a comic book. The splotch paused in front of them, and its edges fluttered, like a kid wiggling her fingers at a choice of candy. Vika blinked as the ink splotch sent a sneaky tendril onto the paper and erased a swatch of red. Then, quickly, as if it couldn't resist, it surged onto the paper and spread out, devouring all the ink and leaving the page blank.

This was definitely the creature she'd seen in Ethan's room that night—and she was positive it must be doing his project for him. It seemed to be doing Mr. Rylance's work, too!

The flatbed scanner made a beep, and suddenly the big monitor behind it lit up, showing the artwork in all its glory. Vika knew that most artists and illustrators, even if they worked by hand, transferred their drawings to computer so they could make more adjustments.

The ink splotch paused and seemed to tense at the sight of the brilliant colors on the screen. Curiously it flowed up the plastic base of the monitor. It wanted a closer look. But when it surged onto the glass screen, it slipped back down so fast it went right off the screen and landed in a tall glass tumbler left on the table.

The splotch tried to climb the sides but only made it an inch or so before sliding back down.

It can't move on glass, Vika thought. *Interesting.*

The splotch churned round and round, seeming very agitated. Vika felt kind of sorry for it, trapped in the glass. It was just sitting right there, ready to grab.

She hurried to one of the French doors and tried the knob. To her amazement, it turned. She opened the door and stepped inside Mr. Rylance's studio. She crept closer to the table.

A hiss made her jerk round. A big old cat was rising from a cushion, its fur spiked.

"What is it, Rickman?" she heard Mr. Rylance say from the hallway, getting closer.

Quickly she retreated, closing the door silently behind her and ducking out of sight. When she peeped up again, Mr. Rylance was looking around his table.

"Inkling?"

It has a name, Vika thought.

Mr. Rylance's frown dissolved into a smile when he spotted Inkling in the glass.

"Stuck?" she heard him say. He tipped Inkling out of the glass back onto the drafting table.

"I see you've had a snack," Mr. Rylance said, nodding at the blank comic-book page. "So. Ready to do some more?"

Imagine, Vika thought, *the things you could make with Inkling.*

• • •

When Ethan got home from school, he found Inkling on his desk, looking pale and small.

"Inkling? What's wrong?"

Listlessly, he wrote:

JUST TIRED.

"What were you doing today?"

HELPING YOUR DAD.

"Really?"

Ethan grabbed his favorite book from his shelf, *Danny the Champion of the World,* and opened it for Inkling. Slowly Inkling pulled himself onto the title page and took a sip of the lettering.

THAT'S VERY REFRESHING. THANK YOU, ETHAN.

Ethan walked straight to his father's studio. Dad was whistling at his drafting table, looking over his work. For just a moment Ethan was so mesmerized by its beauty that he forgot he was angry. Then he turned back to his father.

"I thought you weren't going to use him anymore!"

Dad's eyebrows lifted in surprise. "I needed a little nudge in the right direction. Anyway, he likes to draw."

"He gets tired," Ethan said accusingly. "It's not good to use him so much."

"Haven't *you* been?"

"Not like this! He just *helps* me draw. You must've been using him all day! Did you even feed him?"

Dad frowned. "Um, sure, he had a few comic-book pages."

"That's not enough! And those aren't good for him!" His own anger startled him, but it felt good, too. "You've got to take care of him, Dad!"

He stormed out of the studio and went back to his room to check on Inkling. Maybe he was just as bad as his father, making him work. Inkling didn't seem to mind it, but was he just being nice?

Ethan found Inkling already on page six of the book. His color had returned, and he was eating more quickly.

"Feeling better?" he asked.

YES. THIS IS A VERY GOOD STORY. I LIKE THE ILLUS-TRATIONS, TOO.

Lately, Inkling's way of talking didn't seem so influenced by what he was reading. It was like he'd found his own voice.

Ethan turned as his dad entered the room.

"Hey, I'm sorry, Ethan," he said. "It won't happen again. From now on, nothing but the best for Inkling. The finest stories and artwork. I promise. I already know what to start him off with."

"Okay," said Ethan. "Good, but—"

"All he needs is food and a rest," Dad said. "And he'll be ready to go again tomorrow."

"You're going to *keep* using him?"

"I don't see why not."

Ethan knew he was on shaky ground here. He was using Inkling, too—but not for everything. The story came from Soren, the coloring and lettering were being done by Pino and Brady, and Ethan himself was now doing the drawings—with constant help from Inkling.

"When I got home, it was like he barely had any ink left! It's probably all that color he's using for you."

"We'll make sure he gets lots of color in his food."

YES PLEASE, Inkling wrote on the page.

"But if you keep using him all day, he'll be too tired to help me," Ethan blurted out. How could he ask Inkling to work again tonight? "The artwork's due at the end of the week!"

"Let me give you a hand," Dad said.

"No!" Just days ago he would have jumped at the offer. But he felt differently now.

"I like working with Inkling," Ethan said, and then he realized that neither of them had asked Inkling how he felt about things.

"Inkling, are you okay helping both of us?"

I HAVE PLENTY OF INK TO GO ROUND.

Dad chuckled, but Ethan wondered if Inkling was just being generous. He had a very generous nature.

"There you go," said Dad. "We'll just make sure Inkling

gets plenty of rest. I've got to go pick up Sarah. Come with me and we can walk home through the park?"

• • •

It had been a while since they'd all gone to the park together. The day was overcast, but the trees were flowering, and there were enough new green things pushing their way out of the earth that it seemed bright anyway. They took the paved path that ran alongside the stream.

When he was younger, Ethan had spent a ton of time in the park. Mom had been a big believer in family walks. The park was huge, with lots of stuff to do. There was a castle playground, a little zoo—bison, peacocks, scary emus!—a duck pond, and a café on the hill where you could get chocolate cake. Best of all, in spring, you could find little frogs near the fence by the pond. Mom had been better than Dad at spotting them. They'd catch them in their hands, admire them awhile, and let them go.

Right now, the highlight for Sarah was the dogs. Every one she passed, she asked if she could pat it. She had many questions for the dog walkers. What was the dog's name? Did it shake paws? Could she give it a treat? It was slow going.

"How's your graphic novel project coming along?" Dad asked.

Ethan looked at him in surprise. It was the first time he'd actually asked about it. So he told him about the story Soren had come up with, and Dad chuckled.

"A gorilla secret agent," he said. "I like it. And Inkling's helping with the art?"

"Well, at first he did everything, but I'd make him mess it up a bit. So it didn't look too good. But I wanted to do the rest myself, so he's been teaching me as we go. It's still mostly him, but I think I'm getting better."

He glanced over at his father, hoping he'd say something like "I'm sure you are!" or "You're doing the right thing," but Dad was already looking distracted again and just said, "Good, good."

Up ahead, Ethan saw the toppled tree trunk that had spanned the stream for as long as he could remember. He and his dad used to cross it all the time, while Mom took Sarah across the bridge farther on, to meet them on the other side.

Ethan hadn't walked the tree in a couple of years, but today he hopped onto it. All the steps came back to him, the right places to plant his feet.

Sarah called out, "Ethan, no! Come back!"

"It's okay, Sarah!" he called over his shoulder. He reached the other side. It was easier than it used to be, but still satisfying. When he returned to Sarah, she threw herself into his arms and cried, "She was worried about you!"

Here was the thing about a Sarah hug. It was a real embrace. There was nothing half-hearted about it. Her soft arms folded around your neck, and she pressed her cheek against yours and smushed her body against you, and you felt like you'd just won the most amazing prize. And you couldn't help grinning.

"I'm fine," said Ethan. "It's fun!"

"Sarah wants to do it, too!"

Ethan looked at Dad.

"She won't be able to," Dad said. "Let's cross at the bridge."

But Sarah wasn't happy with that decision and stubbornly planted herself at the end of the trunk.

"I can help her," Ethan suggested. "She's older than I was when I first did it."

"Yes, but . . ."

"Come on, Sarah," said Ethan. For some reason he really wanted Sarah to cross the log. She'd like it. What was the worst thing that could happen? They'd lose their balance and fall a couple of feet into water that wasn't even up to her knees. They'd get muddy.

"She's scared!" said Sarah when he hoisted her onto the log.

"Okay," he said. "We don't have to do it."

Sarah took a deep breath. "Sarah will be brave."

"*I* will be brave," Ethan corrected her.

"Yes, she will be brave," Sarah countered.

"I'm holding on to you," Ethan said, right behind her. He kept his hands on her shoulder and nudged her feet forward with his own. They made it out halfway.

"Just a few more steps!" Ethan told her.

"She's getting closer!" Sarah hollered.

A few times she stopped and said she was scared, and Ethan waited, and eventually they made it to the other side.

"You did it!" Ethan told Sarah.

He looked across at his dad. There was a smile on his face, but he still looked like his thoughts were elsewhere.

"You're really good with her," he told Ethan when he joined them on the other side of the stream.

"Zoo!" Sarah said.

Dad shook his head. "Let's get home. I want to do a little more work with Inkling before dinner. I'm at this tricky part and I just want to see which way the story's going to go. Inkling's probably perked up by now, don't you think?"

"Maybe."

"Tomorrow he's all yours, promise." Dad smiled and ruffled Ethan's hair. "I feel like things are really starting to roll now."

Ethan couldn't help smiling back. It was good to have Dad like this, even if he was lost in his own thoughts. Maybe his own ideas were finally starting to flow—which was exactly what Ethan had hoped.

The whole way home, Sarah talked about Lucy crossing the stream on the big log. And Ethan thought, *Hey, she has a new story to tell, too.*

• • •

In the sleeping house, Inkling hesitated outside the studio.

He was tired. After dinner, he'd done some more drawing for Mr. Rylance, and even after eating, he still felt watery and weak. But that couldn't dull the urgency he felt.

Something to find.

He knew, somehow, that it was in the studio. It was something Peter Rylance needed to see. For a while, Inkling had thought that helping Ethan's dad draw a new graphic novel might be all the help he needed. But he realized that wasn't it—not the kind of thing that would help the *whole* family.

It was in the studio.

But Inkling was afraid to go in. Yes, he was scared of Rickman, and the sketchbook, but he was also scared of what he might find. He remembered the feelings that had flooded him when he drew Mr. Rylance's dreams. So much loneliness and sadness and anger. Was more of that awaiting him?

Inkling shifted nervously on the floor.

Why was everything worse at night? During the day, he could work in the studio with Mr. Rylance. But at night, the idea of the dark space was overwhelming. It was like everything bad that was tamped down during the day broke free and galloped around the house.

His courage failed him, and he turned and slunk back to Ethan's room.

He curled up inside *Danny the Champion of the World,* beside his favorite picture, and wished he were braver.

CHAPTER 13

After school, when Ethan got home, he walked into his father's studio to see Inkling inside a tall glass vase on the drafting table.

"What's this?" he exclaimed.

His father had just torn a page from a nearby art book, rolled it into a tube, and shoved it into the vase.

"Hmm?" he said, looking up. "I'm feeding him. This is an Edward Hopper painting—I want Inkling to get a feel for his streetscapes."

"No, I meant why's he in a *vase*?"

"Oh, it's just easier to feed him . . . ," said his father, a bit guiltily.

Ethan tipped over the vase so that Inkling could flow out onto the drafting table.

HELLO, ETHAN.

"Hi, Inkling," he said. He turned back to his dad. "You can't keep him in a vase!"

"I like to know where he is. And know he's safe."

"You've got him caged up like a prisoner!"

"Don't you think you're overreacting a bit?"

"No!"

"Also, you must've noticed: he's a snacker. You're right, those trashy comics get him all hyper, and then his drawings aren't as good, and then he crashes. This way I make sure he's only getting the good stuff. He had Shaun Tan's *The Arrival* this morning. You liked that one, didn't you, Inkling?"

IT WAS STRANGE AND BEAUTIFUL. THE MAN WAS VERY BRAVE.

"That's great," said Ethan, "but, Dad—"

"And then he just gobbled up *Mortal Engines*," Dad said proudly.

THRILLING! I LOVE THE WAY THE CITIES EAT EACH OTHER!

Ethan raised his voice. "Dad, did you even *ask* him if he liked being in a vase?"

"Ethan, a lot of animals—and people, too—like small, cozy spaces. It makes them feel safe."

Ethan turned to Inkling. "Do you like being in the vase?"

NO. I HATE GLASS.

"See!" Ethan said to his father.

Dad lowered his voice. "I think you're giving Inkling too many human qualities."

"He can hear you," Ethan said.

I MOST CERTAINLY CAN.

"Look, you agree yourself, Inkling sprang from my pen, my ink, my sketchbook—"

At the very word, Ethan saw Inkling tremble.

"—so he's just an extension of my imagination."

"Yeah, but he's *more* than that!" insisted Ethan. "He plays with Sarah and gives her the puppy she wanted, and he gives me drawing lessons, and he's making your new graphic novel because you can't!"

His father's face hardened, but he said nothing. Ethan knew it was a harsh thing to say, but it was true. Inkling was saving them, and his father was treating him like a prisoner.

"And he's my *friend*," Ethan added, more quietly. "You can't keep him in a vase. It's cruel."

"Still, we need to keep him somewhere safer. Like a place where he can't get out."

"He's not an animal, Dad!"

"Maybe not," said Dad, "but we can't afford to lose him. Either of us."

• • •

That night, at the threshold of the studio, Inkling screwed up his courage and slipped inside. He was trembling, but he was on a quest, and he'd read enough stories by now to know that a hero did not fail at his quest.

Even though Ethan had offered him lots of delicious books and artwork earlier, he still felt very tired. Working with Mr. Rylance left him exhausted in a way that not even the brightest colors and crispest text could completely remedy. He was still happy with *Danny the Champion of the World,* but he probably wasn't eating as much as he needed because he was slowly *savoring* the story.

After dinner, he'd told Ethan he could help with his project, but Ethan shook his head and said no, it was okay; he'd rather Inkling just rested. He was a kind boy.

Before gliding deeper inside Peter Rylance's studio, Inkling checked to make sure there was no sign of Rickman. The enticing fragrance of ink swirled from the drafting table, from the crammed bookshelves—but he felt the strongest pull from the big closet to his left. The sliding door was ajar.

Inside were six deep shelves, crowded with all sorts of things. Inkling wished he knew what he was looking for. He meandered around mugs filled with colored pencils and bamboo brushes, shallow dishes filled with gritty erasers and thumbtacks and paper clips. He slithered amongst spray cans, stacks of dog-eared magazines, rolls of tape, unopened bottles of Chinese ink. Reluctantly he dipped into saggy cardboard file folders filled with boring forms and paperwork.

Near the bottom of the closet, things got even messier. He paused. *Go deeper back.* He wended his way past an ancient pencil sharpener, an old camera, and a crusty humidifier. Shoved into the very back corner was a blue plastic bin. Inkling froze. A shiver of electricity passed through him.

Without a doubt, this was it. *This* was what he'd been looking for!

Quaking with excitement now, he poured himself into the open bin. There were reading glasses, a watch, a small zippered pouch, and a couple of paperback books—one that had never been read (the spine was too perfect) and another that looked like it had been read many, many times. It was called *The Secret Garden*.

Jutting from between the pages was the tiniest corner of a piece of notepaper.

It had a kind of gravitational pull—a bit like the sketchbook, but this didn't feel sinister. It felt *necessary*.

Inkling was about to slide closer when a monster uncoiled itself from the closet and pushed its head toward him. Inkling saw two enormous black eyes and fangs in a narrow jaw. He recoiled in terror.

From his resting place, Rickman lunged.

Inkling felt Rickman's claws sink into him, and he made himself as small as possible and slithered free. He went straight up the wall of the closet, slipped out onto the studio ceiling, and flowed into the shadow of the light fixture. Rickman slunk around, trying to find him.

The cat didn't have the stamina to search for long. He

ambled back to the closet, plonked down right in front, and began licking himself.

Defeated, Inkling retreated to Ethan's room.

• • •

In the morning, Ethan still thought Inkling looked wiped out. He chewed at his lip and made a decision.

"You're coming to school with me."

I BELIEVE YOUR FATHER WANTED MY HELP TODAY.

"That's just too bad. You need a vacation. We'll put some good books in my backpack, and you can take it easy."

SHOULD YOU ASK YOUR FATHER FIRST?

"Nope." He knew Dad would be upset when he found out, but he didn't care. "And look . . ." This part was harder to say. "You don't have to help me with my project anymore. You've got enough to do, with Dad."

BUT I WANT TO HELP YOU FINISH IT! YOU ARE MY FRIEND!

"Yeah, but you get so tired and I don't want you . . . getting sick." He felt a sudden tightness in his throat. He remembered the picture of his mother in her hospital bed.

I AM FINE, ETHAN. TRULY. WE CAN FINISH IT TODAY. AT SCHOOL.

"Are you sure? You have to be sure!"

YES! WE'VE REALLY JUST GOT A FEW MORE PANELS TO DO.

"Okay. Thanks, Inkling."

AND, ETHAN, THERE IS SOMETHING LOST THAT YOUR FATHER NEEDS TO FIND. I THINK I'VE FOUND IT—

At that moment, his father called out that breakfast was ready.

"I want to get you hidden in my backpack," Ethan said to Inkling. "Tell me later, okay?"

• • •

Ms. D was going to give them last period to work on their projects, but Ethan thought it was too risky to use Inkling with everyone watching. So he asked his teacher if he could stay in the classroom during lunch to work. That way, he'd have the last drawings ready for Pino and Brady to color and letter.

He took out the final spread. He had the classroom to himself. He got out his markers and reached into his backpack. "Inkling," he whispered. He felt the small breeze as Inkling flowed onto his hand.

He kept his back to the door so anyone peeping through the window wouldn't be able to see Inkling. Then they got to work.

As always, Ethan knew how he wanted these final images to look, but it seemed impossible that his stupid stick figures could ever transform into the pictures he imagined.

Over the days, he and Inkling had gotten faster working together, knowing instinctively which way the other was leaning. Just having Inkling on the tip of his pen gave Ethan confidence. He didn't get paralyzed thinking he'd make a mistake. He took risks. But he also thought, day by day, he was getting a bit better.

As they started the final splash panel, Ethan's heart beat

faster. It was a big sweeping picture of the gorilla looking out over the zoo and city as the sun set, mission accomplished, triumphant. When he finished, he was a bit out of breath, like he'd just run a sprint. It was done.

"Thanks," he whispered to Inkling.

On the edge of the page, Inkling wrote:

YOU DID THAT LAST ONE ALL BY YOURSELF.

"Are you kidding me?"

YOU'VE GOTTEN A LOT BETTER!

Ethan stared hard at the last illustration. In no way was it as good as the others, but it wasn't half bad by comparison. By himself. He stared at the work a bit longer and felt a swell of accomplishment.

A soccer ball hit the window, and when he stood to look, he saw Pino in the schoolyard, waving for him to come join them. There were still a few minutes before the bell.

When he looked at Inkling, he felt a pang of guilt. Inkling didn't look as pale as he had first thing this morning, but he still didn't look his best.

"I brought some good books for you," he said as he slipped Inkling inside his backpack.

THANKS. I'VE STILL GOT A FEW MORE CHAPTERS OF DANNY. I LIKE HOW THEY LIVE IN A GYPSY CARAVAN.

"Me too!" When he was younger, he'd kept asking his parents if they could live in a gypsy caravan and sleep in bunk beds. "Thanks, Inkling, for all your help. You really saved me."

YOU'RE VERY WELCOME, ETHAN.

"Do you want me to leave the backpack a bit open so you get some light?"

NO THANK YOU, THAT'S ALL RIGHT.

Ethan knew that Inkling didn't need light to read or eat or even draw, but he thought it was only polite to ask. He zipped his backpack shut, left it on his hook, and ran out to tell Soren and the others that he was finished.

CHAPTER 14

Ethan had barely kicked off his shoes when his father appeared in the hallway, looking flustered.

"Did you take him to school with you?"

Ethan nodded. "He needed a break."

"So you thought you'd sneak him out without telling me?"

"He was really pale, Dad!"

"I lost an entire day's work!"

"There must've been stuff you could do. On your own."

He shouldn't have said that, especially the last part, because his father's face flushed with anger.

"Ethan, this is my work, and I need to get it done!"

Ethan felt something break free inside him. "But it's not even *your* work! You've got someone doing it all for you. And you don't even care if you kill him!"

His father started to say something, then checked himself and took a breath. "Obviously, I'd rather be doing the work entirely on my own. But I can't right now, all right? I'm still having a lot of trouble."

Dad slumped a little, and Ethan felt some of his own anger leave him.

"He helped me finish my project at school," he told his dad. "But I did the last few pictures on my own."

His dad's smile was weary but genuine. "That's great. I'm proud of you."

Ethan shrugged. "Why? Mostly I cheated."

"Sounds like you tried to make it right, without letting your friends down."

For a moment neither of them said anything.

"I do care about Inkling," Dad said. "And I'll try not to lean on him so heavily. How is he now?"

Ethan unzipped his backpack. "Inkling?"

He put his hand inside and waited for the cool gust against his skin. It didn't come.

"Inkling?"

He opened his backpack all the way, pulled out *Danny the Champion of the World,* and flipped through the last few chapters. Maybe Inkling had fallen asleep. The pages still had words on them, which meant Inkling hadn't read them yet. But there was no sign of him.

In alarm, Ethan dumped everything onto the floor. Textbooks and binders and crumpled handouts and ancient tests and sticky food wrappers. He started sifting through it all but couldn't see Inkling on any of it.

"You didn't keep him in a jar or anything?" Dad asked.

"No!"

"You said he wouldn't run off!"

Would Inkling do that, just run away? An even more terrible thought occurred to Ethan.

"Could he have . . . died?" he asked Dad urgently.

"How could he die?"

"What if he just ran out of ink altogether! It was sort of like blood to him! Maybe we worked him to death!"

"I'll drive you back to school," Dad said. "That's the last place you saw him, right? Maybe he wandered off. You said he did that once before, right?"

Ethan nodded gratefully. "The art room, yeah. Let's go."

• • •

The school hallways were deserted, except for a solitary janitor who pushed a long pink broom, sweeping up a day's worth of crushed juice boxes and plastic spoons and lone sneakers. Some of the classroom doors were still open, including the one to Ethan's homeroom, and he ran inside.

"Inkling?"

He checked in the desks, the bookshelves.

"How would we find him?" his father asked, looking around, bewildered.

"Just look for any movement. Like shadows."

But what if he was too pale and dried up by now? Ethan

thought miserably. *Would he even show up?* He couldn't see any sign of him—no erased book covers or wall posters. Surely Inkling wouldn't have been able to resist them. Was he too weak even to eat?

In the library, he and his dad walked up and down the aisles, but if Inkling was nestled inside the pages of a book, they'd never spot him. Especially if he *wanted* to stay hidden. Maybe he was sick and tired of Ethan and his whole family. Maybe he wanted to be left alone.

Back in the hallway, Ethan asked the janitor if he could unlock the art room, but the janitor said he couldn't unless they had the principal's permission. Ethan cupped his hands and peered through the window, watching for any sign of motion.

"We've got to go pick up Sarah," Dad said.

Ethan was quiet all the way home. It was a miserable evening. Sarah kept calling out for her puppy, Lucy, and didn't understand why she wouldn't come play. Ethan told her that she was gone for just a bit. He hoped he wasn't lying.

• • •

As his jar was finally lifted out of the darkness, Inkling looked all around.

Where was Ethan? This was not his room.

Peering through the glass at him was Vika. Behind her stood a man he'd never seen before.

You greedy idiot, Inkling told himself. *This is all your fault.*

After Ethan had put him back inside his backpack, he'd

been grazing contentedly on his book, enjoying the ink, and especially the story. And then he'd felt himself being lowered to the floor. The top of the backpack opened just a little bit, and a piece of paper slipped inside. He could practically taste the red ink. He left the book and slid onto the colorful piece of paper. So much red! The more he ate, the more he wanted. He swept higher and higher up the paper until he was outside the backpack. Suddenly there was another narrow strip of newsprint before him on the floor, luring him with its comic-book colors.

Like a dark flame, Inkling had crackled across it—and then suddenly knocked against something hard and slippery. Glass! Startled, he pulled back and hit more glass behind him. He spread himself in all directions, but every part of him hit more of the same. Feeling himself tipped and lifted, he realized he was inside a jar with the piece of comic-book paper that had lured him. The top of the jar was screwed tight.

Then he'd been dropped into a backpack—and darkness, until this moment.

"Look," Vika said to the man behind her.

Inkling stayed still on the paper. During the afternoon, he'd nervously eaten all the ink, so the crumpled page was completely blank, except for him.

"Dad, right here," Vika said, pointing at Inkling in great excitement.

Her father squinted. "It's ink spilled on paper."

"It's not normal ink," she said. "I saw this stuff at Ethan's house. This stuff can draw anything!"

"Vika, come on. This is a joke, right?"

Inkling stayed frozen. He could hear the impatience in Mr. Worthington's voice.

"No, I *saw* it! Ethan's been using this thing to draw his project at school. It's like intelligent ink. And I watched Mr. Rylance using it in his studio."

"He showed you this? When?"

"Well, no, I was watching through the window—"

"You were *spying* on him?"

Inkling was glad to hear her father getting angry.

"Dad, just listen! This stuff draws and paints in color. And it's amazing. It was making a new comic book for him."

For a second, her father seemed to forget his anger. "So he *is* working on something!"

"Yeah, but he's not doing it himself! This thing does the work! Look, I'll show you."

Vika moved her face close to the glass. "Draw something, Inkling."

How did she know his name? He stayed motionless on the paper. He didn't like Vika, and he especially didn't like being kidnapped. He needed to get back home. He needed to help Peter Rylance—and not just with his graphic novel. Inkling hadn't had the chance to tell Ethan about what he'd found in the studio closet. He needed to get home and lead them to it.

"I know you can understand me," Vika said. "Draw an octopus, whatever you like."

Why on earth would he draw for them?

Vika's eyes narrowed in anger, and she shook the jar. Inkling held tight to every pore in the paper, but he was afraid he might have shifted a bit.

"Dad, see that?" Vika said. "He's in a different position!"

Inkling froze.

"Looks the same to me," Mr. Worthington said.

"Dad, this thing could draw you an entire comic in one day! Anything you wanted. Those *Exterminatrix* things you were talking about. You said your company needed a hit. This could do it!"

Inkling saw Mr. Worthington's face soften. He touched his daughter's head tenderly. "Honey, you don't need to worry about any of this. The company's going to be fine—"

"That's not what you said to Mom a few nights ago."

He smiled tiredly. "We're fine, all right? Now look, where did you even get this?"

"Ethan's backpack," she mumbled. "He brought it to school."

"I think he's been playing a trick on you, Vika. But that doesn't make it okay to sneak around their house. Or steal. Monday morning, I want you to give this back, okay?"

Inkling waited for her to say yes, but she didn't.

• • •

"Look," Soren said, "let's just go through the steps one more time."

"I've already told you everything!" Ethan said.

It was Saturday morning, and they were sitting on the floor of Ethan's bedroom, eating cookies right out of the package. The cookies were all smashed into little bits because Sarah had been the one to pick them off the supermarket shelf and hurl them into the cart.

"In movies," Soren said, "whenever people retrace their steps, they usually find vital clues. Or, well, get horribly mangled and eaten."

"Okay, fine," Ethan said, and once again told his friend everything that he'd done yesterday since finishing the drawings with Inkling.

"Your backpack," said Soren, nodding at it. "You're sure you checked every pocket?"

"I dumped everything out, yeah." He pointed at the pile on the floor.

"Have you touched it since?"

"No."

"Excellent. So the crime scene is, we can say, uncontaminated."

"Crime scene?"

Soren held out a hand for the empty backpack. "May I?"

Ethan was impressed by Soren's sudden calm command. Soren unzipped every single pocket.

"Now, the inside of your backpack is black, and Inkling is also black, so he could easily blend in."

Soren took out a small penlight. He always carried one in case there was a power outage and he was trapped alone in a threatening environment, like a sewer or an abandoned factory. Carefully he inspected every inch of the backpack.

"Okay, I agree, it looks clean," he said. "Now let's examine the contents."

He shifted his attention to the pile of stuff. It was a big pile. Ethan was not organized. Things tended to stay in his backpack for a long time. When he needed to find something, he just dumped everything out till he found it, then crammed everything else right back in.

Methodically, Soren sifted through the mess. "A Twinkie wrapper with an expiration date of"—he squinted at the wrapper—"nine months ago. A crumpled piece of paper, which is . . . a math test from last month. You got six out of ten, by the way."

"This is a waste of time."

"Another crumpled piece of paper, which is . . . nothing."

Ethan squinted. "Hang on."

This wasn't regular lined paper. It was newsprint. He looked closer. A blank piece of newsprint, about comic-book size, ripped out carefully . . . and there, along the sides, a few traces of red.

"Inkling ate this!" Ethan said. "There was a lot of red and he gobbled it. But I never put this in my backpack! I don't give him comics anymore."

"So what we're saying," Soren began, "is someone *else* put it in there."

"To lure him out!" Ethan exclaimed. "To steal him!"

He looked at his friend and they nodded meaningfully at each other.

"It's got to be her," said Ethan.

"Heather Lee," Soren said.

"What?"

"Come on, she's always looking at you. She's a crazy superfan!"

"What're you talking about? Heather's nice!"

"In movies, it's always the nice people," Soren pointed out. "You think they're nice and then they turn out to be supervillains, or aliens cloaked in human flesh, or—"

"Soren!" Ethan said. "It's Vika, all right. Vika!"

"It seems too obvious," said Soren, sounding a little disappointed. "But yeah, I think you're right."

Ethan couldn't believe he hadn't suspected Vika sooner. Inkling wouldn't just run away. He'd been kidnapped! "She saw Inkling in my bedroom that night, and she's been suspicious ever since! I'm going over there right now!"

"Wait, wait," said Soren. "If you confront her, she'll just deny it."

And she'd get angry, Ethan thought. And when she got angry, she kicked. He was pretty sure she had a few more black belts by now.

"We need another plan," said Ethan.

Soren nodded. "I think I've got just the thing."

CHAPTER 15

Ethan sat on a park bench, nervously digging his fingernail into the chipped paint as he waited for Soren. Most of the park here was grassy and open, but past the fenced dog run there were lots of trees and bushes—right across the street from Vika's house.

Here came Soren now. His steps were jerky because he was carrying a large black case, and it was obviously heavy. He kept switching hands. It was the kind of briefcase that might contain all sorts of things—a trumpet maybe, or a small doomsday device. As he entered the park, Soren glanced nervously all round, which made him look incredibly suspicious.

With a big sigh, he sat down on the bench beside Ethan.

"Mission accomplished?" asked Ethan.

Soren said, "I have the package."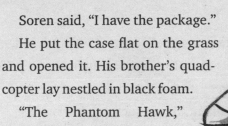

He put the case flat on the grass and opened it. His brother's quadcopter lay nestled in black foam.

"The Phantom Hawk," Soren said reverently. "Its blades are almost noiseless."

"That's good," said Ethan. "We don't want noise."

Soren carefully removed the quadcopter, and Ethan helped him attach a tiny camera to its underside.

"There's an app on my phone," Soren said, "so we can see whatever the camera sees."

Soren switched on the camera and moved the copter around with his hand. On the phone, Ethan could see the image nice and clear.

"Last thing," said Ethan. "Just in case we get close enough." He impaled a single page of a comic book (lots of red) on one of the copter's landing struts. "Good?" he asked Soren.

"Shouldn't affect the aerodynamics," Soren said wisely, taking the controls in his hand.

"It was super nice of Barnaby to lend us this," said Ethan.

"Hmm," said Soren.

"Hang on, he doesn't know you have it?"

"It's fine, it's fine."

"So you're good on how to use this thing?" Ethan asked.

"Yeah, I've . . . he's let me take some test flights."

"How many?"

"One. That he knew about. But I snuck in a few more."

They moved across the park, crouched behind some bushes, and shuffled around until they had a clear view of Vika's house.

"The range is good," said Soren, "and I have clear sightlines of the windows, front and side. You're sure that's her room on the second floor?"

"Pretty sure." Ethan squinted, then smiled. "And the window's open, see?"

"Whoa," said Soren. "Okay. Let's do it. You need to buy me as much time as possible. Keep her downstairs."

Ethan walked across the street to Vika's. It was a nice two-story brick house with a dark green veranda. He marched up the front steps and knocked. It was Mrs. Worthington who opened the door, a sheaf of papers in one hand. Her face lit up with a big smile so warm and genuine Ethan had to smile back.

"Ethan! How nice to see you."

She'd been really kind when Mom was sick; it all came back to him now. She'd left tons of meals for them. She'd also come over to the house several times when Dad needed someone to watch Sarah—and him. He was younger then. She'd played games with them, and made them interesting teas. He'd found her very comforting.

Awkwardly, he stood on the doorstep, tongue-tied.

"Come inside." She shook the papers in her hand. "I've been marking essays all afternoon, but I was just about to make a snack for Vika. I'll tell her you're here."

"Thanks," he said, and followed her into the kitchen.

"Take a seat. Do you like oatmeal cookies? How about some juice? Vika! Ethan's here."

Like her husband, Celine Worthington had no idea that he and Vika were archenemies. How could grown-ups be so clueless?

Ethan sat on one of the stools. This was all going according to plan. He heard footfalls on the stairs and Vika appeared. Just the way she avoided his eyes confirmed his suspicions. Inkling was probably upstairs in her room right now, in some kind of jar.

"Are you two working on a project together?" asked Mrs. Worthington.

"Sort of," Ethan said.

"Vika didn't tell me. But she doesn't tell me much about anything," her mom said lightly, but with a point.

Vika hoisted herself onto the stool opposite Ethan.

"How's it going?" she asked.

"Pretty good," he said.

Through the kitchen window, Ethan could see Mr. Worthington mowing the back lawn. He still had plenty left. Perfect. The noise would cover the sound of the quadcopter. Ethan just hoped Soren kept it away from the downstairs windows.

Vika's mom poured herself a cup of tea. "Well, I need to get back to my fun, fun marking," she said, and returned to the living room.

Ethan nibbled at a cookie. It was a good cookie, but right now it tasted like the stalest cracker in the world.

"How's your project going?" he asked Vika.

He needed to keep her downstairs as long as possible: that was the plan.

"You mean the graphic novel?"

He nodded, taking a tiny sip of juice.

"My part's been done for ages," she said. "I finished over a week ago. The other guys are still coloring and lettering. They better not screw it up."

He nibbled a bit more at his cookie. "Yeah, yours looked really good. I mean, you're the best in the class for sure. I was telling my dad about it. He never said that thing, by the way, about you having no talent. I just made that up."

"I figured," she said.

"So, I was wondering," he said, "if you wouldn't mind giving me some drawing lessons."

She looked at him in total disbelief. "Me?"

"Mm-hmm. I really like the way you draw."

This was completely true. She glanced away as her cheeks flushed at the compliment. In that moment, she looked almost like a . . . normal person. But when she looked back at him, her eyes were narrowed like those of an archenemy.

"Your father's a famous artist. Why doesn't he give you lessons?"

"Too busy."

"Your work looked just fine to me," said Vika. "If it *was* your work."

"So, you *won't* give me lessons?"

"Ethan, why are you here?"

"I think you know why I'm here."

"Mom!" Vika called out. "Ethan's going."

"No I'm not," Ethan said.

Vika smiled coldly. "Take another cookie if you like."

Mrs. Worthington came in, looking surprised. "That was a short meeting. Ethan, say hi to your father for me. And how's Sarah?"

"She's fine, thanks."

He got up from his stool. What else was there to do? He hoped he'd given Soren enough time.

"Bye," he said.

"Vika," Mrs. Worthington said with a tilt of her head, which meant she should see Ethan out.

Vika walked him to the front door.

"Okay, see you," she said robotically.

"Yep. Thanks for the snack, Mrs. Worthington!"

"Anytime, Ethan," she called out from the living room.

The door closed hard behind him. Ethan bolted off the porch and crossed the street to the park. Behind the bushes, Soren sat cross-legged, his eyes flicking from the copter controls in his hand to the phone in his lap to the quadcopter itself—which Ethan could see hovering outside the open window on the second floor of Vika's house.

"It's her room, all right," Soren said. "It's got martial-arts posters all over the walls."

"Can you see Inkling?"

"Not yet. Take the phone. You're my eyes now."

Ethan picked up the phone. On the screen was the interior of Vika's room—everything curvy and a bit distorted from the camera's fish-eye lens. Also, Soren wasn't exactly keeping the copter steady, so it was hard to focus. He knew they didn't have long. Vika might be walking upstairs right now.

"Go inside!" he told Soren.

"What if I can't get out?"

"We have to go inside!"

If Inkling was inside, and they could somehow get close enough, Inkling would grab hold of that bright red comic page dangling beneath the copter. They'd carry him right out.

"But my flight skills aren't—"

A sudden gust of wind rustled Ethan's hair, and on screen the image of Vika's room wobbled violently. When he looked up from the screen, he couldn't see the quadcopter outside the house anymore.

"What happened?" he asked.

Soren's words came slowly. "I am—inside—the—house!"

Ethan looked back to the screen. Everything in Vika's room was now clearer and closer.

"Okay, it's okay," said Ethan.

"I no longer have visual contact with my copter, Ethan!" said Soren, who sounded ready to freak out.

"I'm your eyes now," Ethan told him. "This is good. Just keep her steady. You're doing great."

"What if I can't get back out the window?" Soren squeaked.

"Let's just take a look first. Do a slow circle, turn, turn, keep turning. . . ."

Ethan's eyes were glued to the screen, looking for Inkling while also making sure Soren didn't crash into a lamp or desk or bed.

"I'm flying blind, Ethan!"

"Just a little more to the right now!"

He realized how crazy his plan was. If Vika did have Inkling, would she just leave him out in the open?

"Under the bed?" he said, seeing it right in front of them. "Can you go down low?"

"How low?"

"Lower, lower . . ."

The quadcopter lurched forward and skidded to a halt on Vika's tangled sheets.

"What's happened?" Soren asked, craning his neck to see the screen.

"You've crashed on the bed. It's okay. It's soft."

"I'm going to lift off."

In the bedroom doorway, Vika suddenly appeared.

"Wait!" Ethan said. "Don't move. She's in the room!"

In a high-pitched voice, Soren said, "In the *room*?"

"She hasn't noticed us," Ethan whispered. Luckily, the quadcopter's white body and blades blended in with the sheets.

Ethan's eyes were locked on the screen. Vika closed the door and walked to her bookshelf. She reached behind some books and pulled out an old jam jar. A black shadow swirled round the bottom, trying to climb the sides.

"He's there!" Ethan cried. "He's in a jar!"

Vika tapped on the glass impatiently.

"Looks like she's talking to him," said Soren, leaning closer to the screen. Accidentally he nudged one of the copter controllers. The camera made a little sideways tilt.

"Oh no," Soren breathed.

Vika's head whipped round. She stared right at the quadcopter—

And them.

Vika put down the jar and walked toward the bed.

"Fly! Fly!" Ethan shouted.

Soren jiggled the controls. "Where?"

"Anywhere! Up, up!"

Ethan saw Vika grab for the quad-copter, but it jumped right off the bed, nearly hitting the ceiling.

"Where's the window?" wailed Soren.

"Right, right . . . too far, back to the left . . ."

Vika loomed into view again, this time holding a tennis racket.

"Go, go!" said Ethan. "Left—"

The screen image became a swirl, and Ethan glanced up to see the quadcopter come spinning out of control through Vika's window.

Vika stuck her head out and looked around furiously. "I know it's you, Ethan!" she shouted, and slammed the window shut.

Soren fought to control the damaged quadcopter, and brought it limping back across the street.

"Barnaby's going to kill me," said Soren as he landed it clumsily. One of the rotor blades was crooked.

"It doesn't look too bad," said Ethan.

"It's bad."

"I'll pay for the repairs," said Ethan. "I promise."

At least now he knew where Inkling was.

But he had absolutely no idea how to get him back.

CHAPTER 16

From his jar, Inkling watched as Vika lugged an old fish tank into her bedroom. She cleaned the glass surfaces carefully, then took a moment to stand back and admire her handiwork. She grabbed Inkling's jar, unscrewed the top, and dumped him into the tank.

Still clinging to the crumpled piece of paper, he looked all around. There was no top to this tank. Quick as a cockroach, he darted off the paper and skidded across the glass floor. He hit the wall and, with all his might, strained for the top. He rose only a few inches before sliding back down and spinning helplessly along the bottom of the tank.

Vika was peering in at him. "You hungry?"

A silly question. Of course he was hungry. He was starving! He hadn't had anything to eat since yesterday. He watched as

Vika went to her desk and ripped out a bright page from a comic book. She dropped it into his tank. He climbed onto it like a drowning man hauling himself into a lifeboat. But then he hesitated. It reminded him how he'd been caught, how foolish he'd been. But . . . those colors! That ink! In a second, he'd absorbed the entire page.

"Tasty, huh?" Vika said.

He made no reply. He hadn't said a single word to her.

"Do you want to draw something for me? Please, Inkling."

He peered around the tank. The walls were too high to scale. All the seams were watertight. There was no getting out on his own.

On the piece of paper he wrote:

WHERE IS ETHAN?

He saw her eyes widen at his first written message. Then she looked away guiltily.

"He's not here right now. He loaned you to me for a while."

Inkling felt a pang, even though he knew she must be lying. Ethan would never do that. He was sure he'd heard Vika yell something out the window at Ethan a few minutes ago: "I know it's you, Ethan!" Did that mean Ethan was nearby? Had he tried to rescue him?

IF I DRAW, WILL YOU LET ME OUT?

"Yes! I'll let you out. But I need my dad to see, too."

Inkling didn't trust her, but he had a plan.

Vika disappeared and returned with her father. He was holding a comic book and looked annoyed.

He pointed at Inkling in the tank. "What's all this about?"

"Just watch. Okay, go ahead, Inkling, draw us something wonderful!"

Inkling gathered his thoughts, then whirled into action. He sent out twenty tendrils, all of them drawing on different parts of the paper. He was vaguely aware of Vika and her dad watching in astonishment—and confusion, until finally all the lines and colors met up and they were staring at a double-page spread.

Exhausted, Inkling crouched tensely at the edge of the paper, waiting.

"See!" Vika shouted at her father. "See what it does!"

Mr. Worthington just stared, then started looking up at the ceiling and waving his arm above his head.

"What're you doing?" Vika demanded.

"This is some kind of projection system, right? You're projecting onto—"

"Dad, this isn't a trick!"

To help out, Inkling wrote:

THIS IS MOST CERTAINLY NOT A TRICK.

"I can't believe it . . . ," Mr. Worthington said.

And then he did exactly what Inkling hoped he'd do. He reached into the tank and grabbed the piece of artwork.

"Dad!" Vika said. "Don't—"

But Mr. Worthington had already lifted the paper out of the tank and was peering at it.

Instantly, Inkling darted across the paper and onto Mr. Worthington's hand.

"He's on you!" Vika cried. "He's going to get away!"

"Where'd it go?" Mr. Worthington said, and then spotted Inkling on his sleeve. Vika's dad swatted at him like a mosquito. Inkling darted to his shoulder, then streaked straight down his shirt to his pants, and then off his shoe to the floor. In the distance towered a stack of books—a good hiding place! He bolted toward it.

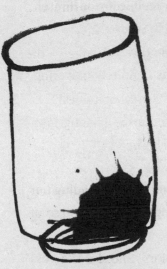

The jar came down on top of him so hard that for a few seconds Inkling couldn't even move. Stunned, he looked at the glass rim surrounding him—and not just surrounding him but . . . cutting *through* him.

Most of him was *inside* the glass, but a small hunk of him was *outside*. Was it even connected to him anymore? Before he could try to slide himself back together, Vika scraped the jar hard across the floor, tipped it right side up, and lifted it into the air.

Inkling slid to the bottom of the jar, still too bewildered to move. But he could see a little severed piece of himself lying lifelessly on the floor! Getting farther and farther away.

Vika screwed on the top and placed the jar on the desk. Inkling kept staring. All he could think about was getting that little piece of himself back! It already looked so pale! Dimly, he was aware of Vika and her father talking, fast and excited.

"This is incredible!" Mr. Worthington said, gazing at the artwork again. "It's so much like Peter's work! How long do you think he's been using this thing?"

"Hey, look at this." Vika knelt down and peered at the small ink splotch on the floor.

"You cut a bit off," her father said, poking it with his finger. It didn't move. "Huh. I think it's dead."

Dead? Inkling felt a strange, hollow feeling inside himself. Pushing against the glass, he strained to see.

"No, look!" Vika said. "It gave a little shiver!"

Inkling had seen it, too. Yes, it was definitely quivering, pale as ink mixed with water.

"It needs food," Vika said.

"Food?" her father asked.

"It eats ink!"

"Wow. Okay. Here, try this," said her father, handing her the comic he'd walked in with. Inkling caught a glimpse of the cover. It said *Exterminatrix*.

Vika found a page with lots of colors. She slid it across the floor so just the edge touched the ink splotch. Inkling watched and waited. The pale splotch didn't move at first, but then shifted the tiniest bit onto the page.

"It moved!" Vika shouted.

Jerkily, the splotch pulled itself onto the page. Vika carefully lifted the comic off the floor, as if she'd just captured a very delicate and rare beetle. She deposited the comic in the fish tank.

At least, thought Inkling, *she's being gentle with it.*

It. Was it an it now? Wasn't it part of him anymore? It was doing something without him! It was eating, and he didn't feel a thing! Something had been taken away from him. It was a small something, but its loss filled him with great sadness.

"It's eating!" Vika said to her father excitedly.

Slower than a snail, the pale splotch moved across the page, leaving a blank trail.

"It erases," said her father.

"Yeah, that's how it eats. And learns, I think. Once it eats something, it knows how to draw it."

"Is that right?" Mr. Worthington went quiet a moment. "So it would be able to duplicate this comic, if it ate it all?"

Vika nodded. "Maybe."

"If it survives," said her dad.

The ink had stopped now, like it was already exhausted.

"It doesn't look quite so pale," said Vika.

Mr. Worthington looked back at Inkling in his jar. "At least that one's fine."

"He tried to escape," Vika said. "I don't think he wants to draw for us."

Mr. Worthington walked closer to the jar and tapped the glass.

Inkling glared back. He wanted to write rude things, but there wasn't even any paper in his jar, and he couldn't draw on the slippery glass.

"If Inkling draws for Peter Rylance," said Mr. Worthington, "I don't see why he wouldn't draw for us, too."

"I'm calling Karl right now," Dad said after Ethan told him that Vika had stolen Inkling. "This is outrageous."

"Maybe she hasn't even told her dad."

Ethan knew how ambitious Vika was. She wanted to be a famous artist. She was already really good, but would she be able to resist using Inkling, and passing the work off as her own? Ethan let out a breath. Just like he'd done. And his own father.

"You think they'll give him back?"

"Of course! It's simple theft." Dad dialed and held the phone to his ear. "There are laws! Intellectual property! The rights of an artist!"

"What about kidnapping!" Ethan added, because Dad didn't seem to be thinking from Inkling's point of view at all.

There was a knock at the door. Beyond the glass window, Ethan could make out Karl and Vika.

"Well, that was easy," Ethan's dad said, putting down his phone and walking to the door.

"Peter," said Mr. Worthington as he and Vika entered the house. "Vika just told me what's going on, and I wanted to set things right."

"I appreciate it, Karl," said Dad.

Mr. Worthington grinned and shook his head. "What an amazing thing!"

"It certainly is."

Ethan watched Vika, trying to figure her out. She was

silent, and her face was serious and closed, like someone who'd just been punished. She had a backpack slung over her shoulder, and he really hoped Inkling was inside.

"So where did it come from?" Karl asked as they all sat down in the living room.

"*He,*" Ethan said. "Not *it*. He came from Dad's sketchbook." He felt like this was his story to tell, since he'd heard it directly from Inkling. "One night, all the ink ran together into a big blob, and he pulled himself off the page."

"Wow," Mr. Worthington said. "If I hadn't already seen it . . . *him* . . . I wouldn't believe a word of this. I couldn't."

"Believe me," said Dad, "I had the same reaction."

"So how long have you had him?"

"Not very long."

Mr. Worthington raised his eyebrows. "You haven't been using him all these years?"

"What?" Dad looked offended.

"Hey, it's okay," said Mr. Worthington, lifting his hands. "Maybe every artist has one of these things, how do I know? I'm just a publisher."

Ethan heard the anger in his father's voice. "I can assure you, Karl, this is a very recent turn of events."

"I'm sorry. It's just that his work looks so much like yours."

"Because he came from Dad's ink!" Ethan told him.

"That makes sense," said Mr. Worthington, but Ethan couldn't tell if he was truly convinced. "So he's come free from the sketchbook and now has a life of his own."

"So it seems," Dad said. He took a breath. "I appreciate you guys coming over." He looked at Vika. "Thanks for bringing him back."

"Oh, we're not bringing him back," said Mr. Worthington.

"What d'you mean?" Ethan demanded. His eyes snapped from Mr. Worthington to Vika, and he now understood the expression on her face: not shame, but cunning.

"So where is he?" Dad asked.

"Somewhere very safe," said Karl. "He's a slippery fellow."

"You kidnapped him!" Ethan shouted. "We want him back!"

"You're talking about him like he's a real person," Mr. Worthington said, smiling.

"Yeah, he is!"

Dad put a calming hand on Ethan's arm. "Karl, he doesn't belong to you."

"But if he's a person, how can he *belong* to anyone?"

Dad sniffed in impatience. "Karl, he came from my sketchbook. He's made of my ink, my imagination!"

"And Vika stole him from my backpack!" Ethan added.

"That may be," said Mr. Worthington, "but it doesn't mean you own him. And maybe Inkling wants to do his own thing now. A change. He drew for you, but he's already drawn for us, too."

A cold surge went through Ethan's veins. Was it true? He'd known Inkling longer than anyone had. Inkling was his friend. He'd said he didn't want to leave. So how could he go and draw for someone else, especially Vika?

"It seems he just likes to draw," Mr. Worthington went on.

"I knew it," Ethan said to Vika. "You just want him to draw for you!"

"As if you don't," she retorted.

"I have bigger plans than that," Mr. Worthington said, "and they include all of us. I see a wonderful collaboration ahead."

"You've got him trapped in a jar!" Ethan said. "I saw it."

"Yes, the spy copter," said Mr. Worthington with a little wince. "I wasn't going to bring that up. That's trespassing and invasion of privacy. You can get in a lot of trouble for that."

"Just like stealing," said Ethan's dad.

"You're very welcome to call the police," said Mr. Worthington.

Ethan and his dad were both silent. He knew how crazy it sounded. They could never go to the police.

"It would make a great headline," said Mr. Worthington. "Blocked Artist Accuses Publisher of Stealing Magical Ink. And even if anyone believed you, then you'd have to fess up that you never actually created your own books."

"That's such a lie!" said Ethan.

Mr. Worthington ignored him. "Peter, I'm not taking Inkling away from you. Of course you can have access to him to finish your project. I'll be moving him to the Prometheus office soon, and you can work with him there. But Inkling never leaves the building. Also, whatever Inkling produces with you will be published by me. As will anything else Inkling might make on his own."

"How's that fair?" said Ethan.

Mr. Worthington scarcely glanced at him. "Ethan, let me and your dad do the talking, okay? Why don't you guys go watch TV."

"No!" said Ethan and Vika at exactly the same time, then glared at each other.

"We want him back!" Ethan said.

"You seem pretty attached to this little guy. And you both obviously have a great working relationship with him. Maybe you can oversee some other projects for Inkling—ones of our choosing, of course."

Ethan saw his father's chest rise and fall heavily. "Karl, we've known each other a long time. We've had a lot of success together—and more than that. You and Celine were so great to us when Olivia died. But this, this is not right."

Mr. Worthington dipped his head thoughtfully and was silent for a moment before saying, "We see things differently, Peter. This is an opportunity for both of us."

"Right," Dad said dubiously.

"We both need Inkling," said Mr. Worthington. "Admit it, Peter: you need him, too. But the brutal truth is, we don't really need *you* anymore. Now that we have Inkling. He's an amazing content creator. Those comics I showed you, the ones you were too high and mighty to do, I bet Inkling won't have any problem doing them."

"He won't do them!" Ethan said. "Not for you!"

"Well, maybe you can help convince him."

"You're stealing, Karl," Ethan's dad said.

"That word again," said Mr. Worthington. "How can you *steal* something that doesn't belong to anyone?"

"Let him out of his jar, then!" Ethan said. "Let him out and see what he does."

Karl smiled calmly at Ethan's dad. "You have my offer. It's a good one. I really hope you take it."

He put his hand on Vika's shoulder, and they stood and let themselves out, closing the door softly behind them.

"They can't do this!" Ethan fumed. He wanted to smash things. He settled for smacking his hand against the wall until it stung with pain. Dad took his hand in both of his to stop him.

"It's not fair!" Ethan said, and realized his face was wet.

"It'll be okay," Dad said. "We'll figure something out."

CHAPTER 17

All through the night, Inkling tried desperately to escape.

He sloshed himself up and down the sides of the jar, hoping to tip it over. But he weighed so little that even when he really got going, the jar barely wobbled. Eventually, Inkling was too tired and seasick to keep going, and he slumped to the bottom, and was still.

Across Vika's bedroom, in the fish tank, the pale little bit of Inkling was still eating its way through a big stack of *Exterminatrix* comics. With every pixel, it grew. It darkened. It became quicker. It gobbled every page clean. There was so much red in the comic—explosions, blood, oh so much blood!—that the splotch actually developed a faint reddish tinge.

When Inkling saw it in the dawn's first light, he was astonished.

It was no longer a feeble little blob, but a sprawling mess. It swelled over the sides of the comic book, like a hairy dude wearing underwear that was too small. It jiggled and jittered. It doodled explosions, and people's heads flying off their bodies, and big blood spatters. It scrawled things like:

BOOM!!!

and

HAHAHAAAAA!!!

and

KERSPLATTCHHHHHUKKKKK!!!

Sometimes a part of the splotch would swell up and pop like an enormous pimple. Other times it sprayed out a spatter of ink, as if it were burping or farting. It was that kind of ink splotch.

Then again, thought Inkling, *what else could it learn from those awful things it was reading and eating all night?*

"Whoa!" said Vika, who'd woken up and was now leaning over the fish tank.

The ink splotch tensed, as if listening.

"Can you hear me?" Vika asked.

In messy lettering it wrote:

UNH ???

"Can—you—hear—me?"

URG!!!

Vika ran out of the room and in less than a minute was back with her dad.

"Look at him now!" she said.

As if showing off his skills, the ink splotch sketched a crazed-looking woman holding a bomb—and then made both explode across the page in a gory mess.

Vika winced, but a smile spread across Mr. Worthington's face.

"Now *that* is definitely a scene from *Exterminatrix*. We have ourselves a very talented artist!"

Watching from his jar, Inkling didn't like what he saw. This creature couldn't have been more different from him. Sure, Inkling liked superhero comics and the occasional explosion, but this was too much. And he felt angry—not at the splotch, but at Vika and Mr. Worthington. They should be feeding this new creature all sorts of things, beautiful books and magnificent artwork. It should have a healthy, mixed diet, like the one Inkling was lucky enough to get from Ethan. Mr. Worthington was going to ruin that ink splotch—and as far as Inkling was concerned, that ink splotch was also *him*. He needed to be reunited with it!

"He can write, too," Vika was saying to her father. "Sort of."
She leaned in close to the tank. "What's your name?"

The ink splotch hesitated. It had only a vague idea what a
name was, and it wasn't really interested in words. Frankly
there weren't that many in these comics. So it tried to write
the words it liked best.

It started with *blood,* then gave up and tried *lots,* and then
had a very half-hearted go at *more.* What ended up on the
page looked a bit like this:

BLOTR

"Blotter?" said Vika.

"It has a certain ring to it," said Mr. Worthington. "I like it."

Very appropriate, thought Inkling.

"Okay, Blotter," said Mr. Worthington, "let's see what you
can do."

From Vika's desk, he took a piece of blank paper and
dropped it into the tank.

"Draw something else for us."

MRE FOD!!!

"What's he saying?" Mr. Worthington asked Vika.

"I think that's *more food.*"

"No, Blotter. First you draw. Then you eat. Lots and lots
of food."

Blotter swelled and belched, then hauled his carcass
toward the blank paper.

And began to draw. His sloppy, inky limbs splattered the
paper. It was the opposite of watching Inkling work. Inkling

was careful and seemed to think about every line, but Blotter was like a garbage truck rumbling down the street, with refuse flying out the back.

And yet, and yet, images began to appear around him, in dazzling color. Inkling couldn't look away. When Blotter was finished, he'd drawn a dark and gruesome spread that was, if anything, more violent than the comics he'd eaten overnight.

"Oh!" said Mr. Worthington. "Oh, *man!*"

Vika swallowed and looked away. Her father grinned like a kid who'd just been told that all the presents under the Christmas tree—not some, but *all*—were his.

"This guy's amazing!" he said. "If he can do a double-page spread this fast, imagine what he can do in a week!"

"I told you!" said Vika.

Her father grabbed her by the shoulders. "And you were right. This is going to be so good!"

• • •

Monday morning, Ethan could barely concentrate on what the teacher was saying. He could only stare at the back of Vika's head, hating her.

At recess, she walked right up to him when he was alone in the yard and said, "Don't even think of trying to steal him."

"That's a laugh. You're the one who stole him from *us.*"

"My dad's home all day, just in case."

"I can't believe you did this," Ethan said, and felt overwhelmed all over again by what had happened. Before he could stop himself, he said, "We need Inkling. Dad needs him, and Sarah needs him. And I need him, too."

For just a second Ethan thought Vika's face softened. But then she said, "Yeah, well, *we* need him, too!"

"How come?"

"Because we need an artist who can actually make comics!"

"My dad's doing one right now!"

She grunted. "Maybe if he'd made one sooner, we wouldn't be in such a mess! My dad could lose his company!"

"What?"

She glared at the pavement. "They're losing money. We could lose our *house!*"

Ethan scowled, not wanting to feel sorry for Vika.

He heard a very happy voice shout his name, and looked up to see Sarah running across the schoolyard toward him. Ethan smiled at the soft impact of her body against his. She threw her arms around him.

Then, to his dismay, Sarah let go and hugged Vika, too.

"Eeka!" she said, beaming up at her.

"Hey, Sarah."

"Lucy is very naughty!" Sarah said. "Be cross with her!"

Vika looked at Ethan. "Who's Lucy?"

"It's what she calls Inkling."

"Oh," said Vika dully.

"She has run away. Naughty puppy! Be cross with her!"

"I hope she comes back soon," Vika said gently, and then looked at Ethan. "Why doesn't your dad just work with us, all together? I don't see what the big deal is."

"Because he's not yours," Ethan said, taking Sarah's hand and walking away. "He's *ours*."

· · ·

All through the day, Inkling splashed himself against the sides of the jar, trying to get Blotter's attention.

Mr. Worthington had placed the fish tank and the jar side by side on the desk in his home office. He came and went, always locking the door behind him.

Before she'd left for school, Vika had sprinkled little bits of newspaper, like fish food, into his jar. She was smart. She wasn't going to stick a big piece of paper down, in case he climbed up and out—which he absolutely would have done. Dejectedly, he ate his little bits of grimy text.

Inkling felt a terrible ache. He missed Ethan. He missed Sarah and wondered how she was doing without her puppy. He even missed Ethan's father a little because, after all, they did share some things in common, like an imagination. And Peter Rylance still needed his help. They all did.

On one of the tiny scraps of blank paper he wrote:
LONELY.

Blotter, meanwhile, was busy drawing. Inkling had to admit, Blotter was an excellent mimic, and bewilderingly fast. Mr. Worthington kept putting fresh paper into his tank, and when Blotter filled it, he'd get rewarded with a few more pages from some vile comic book.

On his biggest bit of paper Inkling wrote:
HELLO!

He kept writing it over and over again, in different-colored letters, hoping Blotter would notice. At last Blotter lurched around and moved closer to the side of his tank. On the paper he wrote:

UNH???

He still didn't have a very good vocabulary. Inkling wrote:

I'M INKLING!

Blotter wrote back:

WHATR YU?!?

SAME AS YOU! Inkling wrote. **IN FACT, YOU ARE ME!**

It took him a while to write this because the paper was so small he had to erase words to make room for the next ones. Maybe Blotter had already lost interest, because he heaved up some ink, like a cat hacking up a hairball. Finally, he coughed up a few more letters.

IM ME!!! said Blotter.

YES, Inkling wrote. **BUT YOU CAME FROM ME.**

Blotter didn't seem too thrilled with this news. He just farted ink and wrote:

NAH!!!

Inkling couldn't figure out how to convince him of this, so he wrote:

WE NEED TO ESCAPE!

Escape was a word Blotter actually understood. In these comics, people were always escaping from monsters and machines and other people who were trying to kill them. In his messy writing, Blotter wrote:

WY???

WE DON'T BELONG HERE, Inkling said. **THIS ISN'T OUR HOME.**

HOM???

THE PLACE WE'RE SUPPOSED TO BE.

I LIK IT HRE!!! Blotter replied.

NOT ME, Inkling said.

THEY PUT YU IN A JR!!!

YES, wrote Inkling. **AND I WANT OUT. HELP.**

Surely this other creature would help him. Blotter had come from his very own ink! And even if Blotter didn't want to be reunited, at least Inkling could be a good influence on him and make sure he ate more nourishing things.

Blotter seemed to be mulling things over, and Inkling became more hopeful by the second. Then Blotter wrote:

WHN SOMEONE'S IN A JR, THEYR IN A JR FOR A REE-SON!!!

This was a very long sentence for Blotter, and it pretty much tired him out. He retreated and sat around bubbling and oozing for a bit. Then he got back to work, drawing another terrifying spread for Mr. Worthington.

Inkling sighed and wondered if Ethan would come looking for him ever again.

CHAPTER 18

"She does not like it," Sarah said, pushing away the robotic dog she'd gotten for her birthday.

Ethan had been trying to get her interested in it while Dad did the dishes after dinner. He patted it. He praised it when it opened its mouth or wagged its tail. But Sarah just watched disdainfully.

"She only wants Lucy," she said, and then, to Ethan's utter surprise, began to cry.

Her eyes crinkled shut and small tears leaked out. She pushed her face into his shoulder and made little crooked moaning sounds. He held on to her.

Sarah hardly ever cried. So when it happened, it was a big deal. It tore at his heart. He hadn't seen her like this since after Mom had died. She hadn't cried right away. She hadn't really understood. She just kept asking the same questions.

Where was Mom? When was she coming home? Why wasn't she coming home?

Week after week, he and Dad had tried to explain that she wouldn't be coming home, that she got sick and died and was gone forever. It had been so awful to have to repeat these things over and over, each word and sentence like a wound reopened.

Eventually, Sarah had stopped asking where Mom was, and didn't talk about her for a while. But then one night at bedtime, she'd just unexpectedly asked for Mom, and cried and cried.

That was one of the worst days Ethan could remember—and he thought about it right now, with Sarah's hot face smushed against him.

With Inkling gone, the house felt empty all over again. All day at school, Ethan had been trying to think up some plan to rescue Inkling. He'd come home to find Dad in his studio, staring blankly out the window. His markers were all capped. On his drafting table, not a single new panel or sketch or line had been added to Inkling's artwork. A sad, invisible weight sagged down over the room.

"We'll find her," Ethan told Sarah now. "I promise."

"What's wrong?" Dad asked, coming in from the kitchen, a dish towel over his shoulder.

"She misses Lucy," Ethan told him.

Dad leaned in and tenderly put his hand on Sarah's head. Sarah lifted her face away from the wet patch on Ethan's shirt and transferred herself into Dad's arms.

"Come on," he said, "let's get you into your pajamas and read some stories."

"O-kay," Sarah said shakily.

Ethan watched her being carried away, sniffling, and knew he absolutely had to keep his promise to her.

• • •

"I've got a plan," Ethan told his dad after Sarah was asleep. "Mr. Worthington said he'd be moving Inkling to the Prometheus Comix office, right?"

Dad nodded. "It's the safest place for Karl to keep him."

"We break in and get him out."

"Ethan—"

"I'm serious. We all need Inkling. We need him back!"

"Agreed, but it's not so simple. You need a key to get into the building, and then a passcode for the actual office. I'm sure it's alarmed."

"We go in through a window," Ethan persisted. "Glass cutter."

"It's on the fourth floor!"

"There's a fire escape, though, right?"

"Ethan, stop. I've been thinking, too. And I have a plan."

"You do?" Ethan felt a flooding relief. His dad's plan would probably be better than his.

"I'm going to call up Karl and accept his offer."

For a moment, Ethan couldn't speak. "What kind of plan is that?"

"Listen. I'd get to work with Inkling—"

"While he's locked up!"

"Yes, but at least that way I'll get to finish my book."

Ethan felt a clutch of disappointment at his heart, then anger.

"Yeah, I guess that's all you care about!"

"We need the money!"

Ethan knew this was supposed to shut him up and make him feel bad. But he didn't feel bad, and he wasn't going to shut up. If Dad was so worried about money, he should've been working harder the past couple of years! He should've been doing *something*. That was his job.

"What about Sarah? She's really upset."

"She'll be fine. She was just tired tonight."

"And how about Inkling?" Ethan demanded. "They want to use him like a printing press! They're going to kill him!"

"If I work with him, I can at least make sure he's properly fed and not getting too tired—"

Ethan sniffed. "Yeah, like *you* were employer of the year."

His father let this one go. "And most important, if I'm working with him, there might be a chance I can smuggle him out somehow."

"That's true," Ethan said, feeling a bit better.

He didn't like to think about going so long without Inkling. He'd become such a constant and cheerful friend. Ethan chewed at his lip. He hated the idea that Inkling might now be friends with Vika, that he was happily drawing for her, his old home already forgotten.

"You've got to promise me," Ethan said to his father, "the first chance you get, you'll rescue him."

• • •

By the end of the day, Blotter had finished an entire comic, and Mr. Worthington was overjoyed.

"It's like a mash-up of all the things I've been feeding him," he told Vika in his home office. "He ate every single issue of *Exterminatrix* and all the copycat bestsellers I could get my hands on. But what he drew is different enough that we can call it our own!"

"Can I see?" she asked.

Dad had turned all the spreads facedown on his desk when she'd walked in.

"Not for your age group," he told her.

Watching from his jar, Inkling had seen the whole thing being drawn. It wasn't just that it was violent and crudely drawn; it was also embarrassingly dull-witted and, well, boring. Inkling had eaten enough books and comics by now to be a pretty good judge of stories and artwork.

"Maybe if you fed him something different," Vika said, as if reading Inkling's mind, "he could do other stuff. Maybe stuff for kids."

"Something to think about down the line, absolutely," Dad replied. "But right now, there's a market for this, and it seems like Blotter can make one every couple of days."

He went dreamily quiet, as if doing math in his head.

"Did Mr. Rylance call?" Vika asked.

"Not yet. It's a shame, but even if he says no, we've got our very own artist in residence here."

"So we're going to be okay?" said Vika. "Your company and everything?"

"With Blotter here, we're going to be rich!"

He looked over at Inkling, who had been watching and listening to all this from his jar.

"What about you, Inkling? Are you ready to draw today?"

Inkling said nothing.

"If you draw, we'll give you some books to eat. Whatever you want."

Still, Inkling remained silent. He wanted nothing to do with this fellow.

"Suit yourself," Mr. Worthington said.

Vika went closer to his jar. "You're looking pale, Inkling. You should eat something."

She looked genuinely concerned, and Inkling's feeling about her shifted a little. She wasn't as bad as her father. She began to tear up more humiliating little bits of newsprint to sprinkle into his jar, but her father stopped her.

"No. If he doesn't draw, he doesn't eat."

Vika frowned. "Dad, he might die!"

"He won't die. Let him get good and hungry. In my experience, the hungrier an artist is, the more creative and productive he gets." He chuckled. "And if he still doesn't draw, maybe we should feed him to Blotter."

At these words, Blotter surged across the fish tank and hit

the wall with such force that the entire tank actually shifted slightly. His inky body boiled high up the glass.

In jagged letters Blotter wrote:

YES!!! GIVE HIM TO ME!!!!!!

"I was just kidding, Blotter," said Mr. Worthington.

Vika asked, "You'd really eat him?"

YES YES YESSSSSSS!! I WNT HIS INK!!!

Watching, Inkling got a seasick feeling inside him. When that little bit of him had been cut off, all he could think about was being reunited with it. Even when Blotter had emerged from his first night's feeding as a bloated thug, Inkling still wanted to absorb him back.

But now he wondered who would absorb whom. Blotter was much beefier and stronger, by the looks of it. And what kind of creature would they be afterward anyway? More Blotter, or more Inkling?

"Interesting," said Mr. Worthington. "Maybe if we combined the two of you, we'd get a superartist." He raised his eyebrows ominously at Inkling. "Something to think about, huh, Inkling? Convince me that I still need you."

After Mr. Worthington left the room, Vika went up to the jar.

"Come on, Inkling, you better draw something."

She actually sounded worried, and that made Inkling worried. He shuddered and wondered if any part of him would survive if Blotter got hold of him.

CHAPTER 19

Outside during recess, Ethan was tossing his banana peel into the compost bin when suddenly Vika was beside him. She looked flushed and a bit out of breath, and Ethan wondered if she was planning on blasting him into a garbage can again.

"I don't really want to talk to you," he said, and turned away.

"Wait." She dug into her pocket and pulled out a crumpled piece of paper and a key. "Here."

Ethan blinked. "What's this?"

"The key to my dad's

building, and the passcode to the office. He's moving Inkling there today."

Incredulous, Ethan stared at her. "What're you doing?"

"I'm helping you get him back, dimwit!"

"Why?"

"I'm worried about him. There's another one now."

Ethan shook his head. "Another one? From where?"

"Inkling. I cut a bit off of him—"

"You *what*?"

In the schoolyard, people looked over, including Soren and Heather Lee.

"By accident!" Vika hissed, shooting him a fiery glance. "And we gave the little picce food and it grew. A lot. He's called Blotter. My dad likes him because he draws for us. Inkling won't."

Ethan felt a flush of happiness. Inkling had stayed loyal to them! He didn't want to be there!

"Anyway," said Vika. "Dad says if Inkling doesn't draw, he doesn't get food." Her mouth wrinkled up a bit. "And if he still refuses, he might get fed to Blotter."

"Blotter would *eat* him?" Ethan said in horror.

Vika nodded. "I think so."

The banana felt suddenly heavy in his stomach. This was a lot to take in. "Okay." He reached for the key and paper in her hand.

She pulled back. "You have to promise me, though. Promise you'll leave Blotter for us. He's going to make those comics my dad wanted. We need him."

"Fine. I don't care," said Ethan. "As long as we get Inkling back."

Vika pressed the paper and key into Ethan's hand. "He's in the supply room. Good luck. Give the key back to me tomorrow, okay?"

She started to walk away.

"Vika," Ethan called after her. "Thanks."

He hurried over to Soren and dragged him to a deserted part of the yard.

"What's going on?" his friend asked, wide-eyed.

Ethan told him everything. "So I'm going to have a sleepover at your house tonight. We'll sneak out. We've got a rescue mission."

Soren stared into the distance, unblinking. "Nighttime. A dark building. Dangerous, gooey creatures."

"You okay with this?"

His friend nodded slowly. "I think I've been waiting for this moment all my life."

• • •

In a strange room, in a locked cabinet, in a glass tank, Inkling knew it was only a matter of time before Blotter ate him.

Right beside his tank was Blotter's. On the bottom were two blank pieces of illustration board, and just a few scraps of comic book that had been devoured long ago. Mr. Worthington said he'd keep Blotter hungry at night, and if he produced well, he'd get a big feed in the morning.

STLL HUNGRY!!!! he scrawled in pointy letters.

Inkling had already searched every corner and seam of his tank for gaps or cracks, but he tried again now with the same result: there was nothing he could squeeze through. He couldn't climb the walls, too slippery and high. And he was getting weaker. Since he'd been moved into this new room, Mr. Worthington had sprinkled only the tiniest scraps of comics for him. And he'd left behind two blank pieces of illustration board, same as for Blotter.

"Draw me something, Inkling," he'd said. "Last chance."

HUNGY!!! Blotter scribbled now. He swelled across the tank and pressed himself against the glass wall closest to Inkling.

Suddenly Inkling felt himself dragged closer. He fought hard to back away. Had Blotter felt it, too? They'd never been placed this close to one another. It was like a magnetic pull. Was this their bodies trying to reunite? Right now, it was a horrifying idea to Inkling.

EET!!!

HE'LL BRING MORE AFTER YOU DRAW, Inkling wrote, trying to calm him.

NO DRAW!!! HUNGY NOW!!!

Blotter backed up and then slammed himself against the glass, hard. His inky body boiled halfway up the side before sliding down.

YU FOOD!!!!!

Inkling retreated to the far end of his tank, quaking.

Blotter gave himself a bigger running start and crashed

against the glass wall again. Inkling felt the shudder through his own tank. This time Blotter climbed higher, just a few inches shy of the top of the tank.

It wouldn't be much longer now.

• • •

Ethan had visited the Prometheus Comix office a few times over the years, but never at night, when it was dark and deserted. It occupied the entire fourth floor of an old warehouse. The high ceiling was lost in shadow. The big windows let in a pale wash of light from the street. Amongst the workstations stood giant cardboard floor displays of the company's most popular characters—most of them from the Kren series. In daylight they were colorful and fun, but now they loomed like sinister sentinels.

"No flashlights," Soren reminded him as they made their way deeper into the office. The windows had no curtains or blinds, so someone outside might notice a flashlight beam.

Ethan wasn't sure where the supply room was, but he guessed farther back. He should have asked Vika. He led them past empty cubicles with swirling screen savers and rows of bobble-headed toys that rocked creepily back and forth.

Soren wore a black tuque, which Ethan thought was unnecessary. It made him feel like a burglar, even though technically they hadn't broken in. They'd used Vika's key to get inside the building, taken the elevator to the fourth floor, and opened the office door with the passcode. His stomach gurgled nervously.

Soren grabbed his arm and he jerked. "What?"

"What if it's all a setup?" Soren whispered. "She gives you keys, but once you're inside, the cops are waiting. We get arrested and thrown in jail!"

It was a terrible thought, but he shook his head. "Vika seemed legit."

"Okay," said Soren, though he didn't sound entirely convinced.

Beyond the workstations was a long hallway. There were no windows here, so Ethan took out his flashlight. Soren took his out, too. It was smaller and more powerful, as befitted someone who was always ready for the end of the world. Their twin beams illuminated several doors. The first few were bathrooms, but the one at the end wasn't marked. Ethan turned the knob and swung the door open.

Shelves rose floor to ceiling against the walls. Some held books and comics; others held reams of paper and toner cartridges and bottles of ink. So many bottles. Along the floor were stacked boxes, still taped shut.

He slipped inside with Soren. Behind them the door whispered closed and clicked.

"Where do we start?" Soren muttered.

"There."

With his flashlight he picked out a deep metal cabinet against the back wall.

"Mr. Worthington wouldn't keep Inkling in plain view, would he? He'd hide him from his workers, right?"

Soren rattled the cabinet's locked doors.

"She didn't give me a key for this," Ethan said. The back of his neck prickled. Maybe Soren was right, and this was all a setup. In the distance he heard a police siren and looked at his friend in alarm, but the sound soon faded away.

Soren flicked the metal doors. "Not so thick," he murmured. "Probably not a deadbolt." From his pocket he took a thick army knife. He opened one of the attachments that looked like a nail file.

"You're pretty good at this stuff," Ethan said, impressed.

Skillfully, Soren slipped the file between the doors, jiggled, and then lifted gently. Something clicked, and the cabinet creaked open.

Ethan shone his light inside. On the middle shelf, side by side, were two big glass tanks. From each came a dark flash of movement.

"Inkling?"

Ethan looked from one tank to the other. In both were a couple of pieces of blank illustration board and a medium-sized ink splotch.

"Which is Inkling?" Soren whispered.

In the left tank, the ink was bouncing around excitedly and quickly writing on the board:

ETHAN! YOU CAME BACK!

"Hang on," said Soren, and shone his flashlight into the right tank. The other ink splotch was also writing:

ETHAN! IT'S ME!

"Oh no," Ethan murmured, swinging the light back to the left tank, where the ink splotch was now writing:

HE'S LYING! I'M INKLING!

"I think he's in this one," Ethan said. "Vika said they weren't feeding him. He hardly has any food in his tank!"

"Neither does this one," Soren pointed out. "And he hasn't drawn anything. Did you say Inkling refused to draw?"

"Neither of them has drawn," Ethan said, checking.

The ink splotch in the right tank was now writing hurriedly:

HE DRAWS AT NITE! HE JUST HASN'T STARTD YET!

Ethan frowned. It wasn't like Inkling to make spelling mistakes anymore, but he *was* writing very quickly.

At the exact same time, both ink splotches wrote:

ETHAN, IT'S ME! ETHAN, IT'S ME!

"Okay," Ethan asked them, "what's the name of my cat?"

Both ink splotches quivered but made no reply.

"Why aren't you writing?" Ethan demanded.

The splotch on the left wrote:

IF I START WRITING, HE'LL COPY ME!

Ethan grabbed a file folder from a shelf and slid it between the two glass tanks. Now Inkling and Blotter couldn't see each other.

"There," he said. "Go!"

Right away, the splotch in the left tank wrote:

RICKMAN!

In the right tank, the splotch swirled and fumed.

"Don't you know?" Soren asked him.

Blotter swelled and belched ink against the side of the tank.

BLAAAAAAARG!!! WHT A STUPD QUESTN!

Only now did Ethan notice the slight red tinge in this splotch's darkness. Farting out little bits of ink behind him, Blotter propelled himself around the tank and slammed against the side.

GIMME MRE FOOD! HUNGY!!

Ethan wrinkled his nose—he felt like he could almost *smell* Blotter. Ethan turned away from him, reached down into the left tank, and lifted out the board with Inkling on top.

THANK YOU, ETHAN, THANK YOU FOR COMING TO GET ME!

"Sorry it took so long."

Inkling slid eagerly onto his hand, and Ethan felt the familiar and strangely comforting cool breeze against his skin.

In his tank Blotter was writing in huge, angry red letters:

HEY! HEYYYY! HE'S MINE! MY FOOOOOD!!!

Ethan felt Inkling quake against his skin. "Let's get out of here."

"Yeah," Soren said, but he kept his flashlight on Blotter's tank, because the ink was swelling and growing, like squid ink filling an aquarium.

"Uh-oh . . . ," Soren squeaked.

Ethan turned back. Blotter hurled himself against the sides of the tank, back and forth, and on the fourth try, his inky body crested the side.

Like a huge tentacle, Blotter flung himself out of the tank and across the room. Ethan tried to track him with his flashlight but lost sight of him when he hit the shelves.

"Can you see him?" he asked Soren.

Their beams darted frantically.

"No! Come on, let's go!"

Soren ran, Ethan at his heels, slamming the storage-room door behind them.

Racing through the dark office, Ethan kept looking back over his shoulder. He had a terrible creeping feeling at the base of his skull. Blotter was just ink, only ink. But he'd never forget what Inkling could do if he got onto your face.

He rushed past a life-sized floor display of Kren, and all the shadow suddenly poured off it and puddled on the floor in front of him.

"Blotter!" he shouted, swerving into the office kitchen.

The oily mass boiled toward him, swirled round his shoe and then up his ankle.

Blotter's touch wasn't a cool gust like Inkling's. It was a hot, clammy hand.

"Soren! He's on me!"

He knew what Blotter really wanted. Inkling. He wanted to eat him! Ethan slammed his hand down on the counter near the sink and whispered, "Inkling, get off me! Hide!"

The moment he saw Inkling's shadow on the counter, he stepped clear. Blotter swirled up his leg like a sweaty tornado.

He smacked at Blotter, and Soren did, too, but the red-tainted ink just swelled past their fists and fingers.

"How do we get him off?" Soren asked helplessly.

"I don't know!"

Blotter covered so much of him now. When the ink reached his jacket, Ethan quickly shrugged it off and tossed it to the floor—where it grazed Soren's shoe. In a second Blotter surged up Soren's leg and encircled his chest.

"It's on me! It's on me!" Soren bellowed, his eyes wider than ever before. He swatted uselessly at the swirling shadow.

In desperation, Ethan grabbed a spray bottle from the kitchen counter and squirted it at Blotter. A blast of cleaning fluid hit Blotter and made him pause. A tiny little bit of him began to drip down Soren's leg.

"I think it works!" Soren said.

Ethan sprayed again, and again, but he got too close, and Blotter leapt onto the bottle itself and poured across it.

Ethan hurled it across the office, but he was too late. Already Blotter was on his hand, his arm, his shoulder.

Then his face.

"He's—" Ethan shouted, but was silenced because his mouth was covered, and seconds later his nostrils.

He couldn't take a breath.

He couldn't let one out.

He couldn't make a sound.

Ethan felt like he was going to explode and crumple all at once.

"Blotter! Stop it!" Soren was shouting, and to Ethan it sounded a long way off because Blotter must've been covering his ears now, too.

He flailed around, swatting himself as if he were being swarmed by hornets.

All he could think was, *Breathe, breathe.*

But he couldn't.

• • •

Inkling saw Ethan stagger against the kitchen counter, Blotter covering his head like an executioner's mask.

Inkling surged toward them. It was easy to get Blotter's attention. The closer he got, the more Inkling felt that strange magnetic force trying to pull them together. Blotter must've noticed it, too, because he seeped off Ethan's face to his shoulder.

Ethan gasped, looking wildly around, his hands flying to his face.

Inkling's attention was fixed on Blotter as he oozed down Ethan's arm toward the counter. Inkling retreated and bumped into a big cleaning sponge. It started to slurp him into its yellow foam, but Inkling fought hard and pulled away.

He looked back. Blotter swirled around Ethan's waist,

building up speed, and then flung himself through the air right toward Inkling.

Inkling was speedy, and he darted out of the way. Blotter landed right on top of the sponge. Before he could flow across it, he was slurped down like someone in quicksand. The yellow sponge turned a dark reddish black.

"He's trapped in the sponge!" Soren shouted, pointing.

"Come on, Inkling!" Ethan said.

Inkling surged across the counter onto Ethan's outstretched hand, and moments later he was in the cozy safety of Ethan's pocket. He knew the boys were running, then felt a jarring thud as Ethan tripped and fell.

"You okay?" he heard Soren ask, and felt Ethan hauled to his feet.

More running. A door swooshing shut behind them, pounding footfalls on stairs, another door, and then he was outside in the cool night air.

CHAPTER 20

Ethan cycled with Soren through the deserted nighttime streets of their neighborhood. When he reached the turn to his house, they stopped their bikes.

"Mission accomplished," Soren said.

"Thanks, Soren."

"Try not to lose him again," his friend said as he pedaled away.

Ethan headed home. He could've gone back to Soren's and slept over, but he was too excited. He wanted to be in his own house, and tell Dad.

He let himself in with his key and turned on the lights in the living room. Reaching his hand into his pocket, he felt the cool gust of Inkling and lifted him out. He put him on the coffee table.

HOME, Inkling wrote.

"Yeah," said Ethan. "Are you okay? Can I do anything for you? Get you something to eat?"

I'M FINE FOR THE MOMENT.

"You sure?"

YES.

Ethan heard the click of his father's bedside lamp, then his father's tread down the hallway. He appeared, squinting and rumpled, in his bathrobe.

"What . . . um . . . what's?" he asked in confusion.

Ethan pointed at the coffee table.

GREETINGS, MR. RYLANCE!

"How?" was all his dad managed to say.

When Ethan had told him the whole tale, Mr. Rylance leaned back in the sofa and had a good scratch of both sides of his head, as if this might help him wake up and think better.

"That was a crazy, risky thing you did," he said. "But you pulled it off!"

"They can't get him back either!" Ethan said. "What're they going to do? Call the police?"

His father sniffed. "No. We just have to make sure we keep Inkling safe so no one can steal him again. It's so good to have you back, Inkling!"

Ethan thought he heard genuine affection in Dad's voice. That was a first. And he thought how happy Sarah would be in the morning when she saw her beloved Lucy.

On the table Inkling was writing:

THERE IS SOMETHING I NEED TO SHOW YOU.

"It's late," said Dad. "Can you show us in the morning?"

I WOULD RATHER DO IT NOW.

Ethan looked at his dad, who nodded. It seemed pretty important to Inkling.

IN THE STUDIO. WATCH OUT FOR RICKMAN, PLEASE.

Ethan chuckled. "Okay."

He let Inkling flow onto his hand and walked down the hall with his father. Inside the studio, he flicked on the light. Rickman stirred on his favorite chair, then buried his head in his paws and closed his eyes. On Ethan's hand, Inkling wrote:

THE CLOSET. THE VERY BOTTOM SHELF. BACK RIGHT CORNER.

Ethan slid the door aside and knelt down.

THE BLUE PLASTIC BIN.

When he glanced at Dad, he was startled by how pale his father was. He stood very still, as if dreading something.

"You know what's in here?" Ethan asked.

His dad just nodded.

Ethan saw the blue bin and pushed stuff out of the way so he could lift it out. He set it on the floor. Inside was a scattering of things, and he had a sickening suspicion of what they were.

"Is this Mom's stuff from the hospital?"

"Yeah."

"Why're you showing us this, Inkling?" Ethan demanded.

WAIT.

Inkling flowed off his hand and headed straight for the

battered paperback copy of *The Secret Garden*. Ethan knew it was one of Mom's favorites. She'd read it to him once long ago when he was sick. She'd said when she was little, she read it whenever she was ill, and it always made her feel better.

Inkling flowed onto the book's spine and with a slim tendril pointed at the tiniest corner of something sticking out between the pages.

"What is that?" Dad asked, bending and taking hold of the book. When he opened it, a small, handwritten note fluttered to the floor.

Ethan stared, but didn't touch it. The writing was Mom's.

Dad picked it up, inhaled, and then pressed it between both palms, like he wasn't ready to read it quite yet.

"You've never seen that?" Ethan asked.

Dad shook his head. "Afterward," he said, his voice thick, "when I had to go and clear away her things, the nurses had already put them in a storage bin, and I never looked at any of it. I just couldn't. I shoved it into the closet. But I don't know how I missed this."

Then he sat down on the floor and read it.

Ethan wanted to read it, too, but it didn't seem right. Instead, he watched his father's face. After a few moments, Dad began to cry silently, and when he was finished reading, his mouth was open, like he wanted to breathe but couldn't.

Instinctively Ethan went and clung onto him, and squeezed hard, like he was trying to keep him from flying apart. Dad shook with terrible, hoarse sobs. Ethan held tighter, and felt the firm weight of Dad's arms, hugging him back.

After a moment, Dad pulled away and got a box of tissues from his desk. He blew his nose, took another to wipe his face.

"I wasn't there when she died," he said. "She was alone."

Ethan had never heard about this. He thought of that terrible picture Inkling had drawn, of Mom by herself in the hospital bed. The image that had been haunting Dad's sleep.

"It was sudden," Dad said. "I'd been at the hospital most of the day, but you guys were at home, and the babysitter had to leave, and I couldn't find anyone to take over. So I came home, and after you were in bed, I just fell asleep. It shouldn't have been like that."

"What did the note say?" Ethan asked.

His father took a moment before answering. "Toward the end, I was just angry with everything. I was worried about you guys, and how we'd be without her. I was all twisted up. I worried she might think I was angry with her. I wanted to make sure she knew I wasn't, and that I loved her, but I didn't even get a chance to say good-bye properly."

Ethan waited. His father nodded at the note.

"I worried about it so much. But she already knew. She understood everything, even things I didn't."

Ethan couldn't stop himself from reading the last line of the note. The handwriting was crooked and faint.

You have so many wonderful stories to tell, but please don't forget the most important story of all, going on under our own roof.

When Ethan looked up, his father was watching him tenderly. "Haven't been doing such a great job, have I?"

Ethan didn't know what to say. On the floor, Inkling wrote: **YOU WERE JUST STUCK.**

Dad read the message and gave a small laugh. There was no bitterness in it, just relief. "Yeah. *Stuck.* That's it exactly. Thanks, Inkling."

CAN I READ THE SECRET GARDEN?

Ethan smiled. "Absolutely."

He was about to stand when something dark oozed out from underneath his sneaker.

"Dad . . ." He pointed, fear jolting through him. "It's Blotter!"

Frantically he kicked off his shoe. Blotter darted across the floor like a huge rat and disappeared into a far corner of the studio. Ethan let Inkling flow onto his hand, then scrambled to his feet and stood beside Dad.

"He must've gotten onto my shoe!" Ethan said. Back at the office, Blotter must have pulled free of the sponge and caught up to him. When he fell, probably.

From his chair, Rickman stood up and hissed.

"Where is he?" Dad croaked, peering into the shadows of the studio.

"He wants to eat Inkling!"

"How do we stop him?" Dad asked.

"Water!" Ethan said. "Lots."

"I'll get a bucket," said Dad, running for the kitchen.

Shadows seeped suddenly up all four walls, throwing the room into twilight even though the overhead light was on. Blotter was huge. He coated the walls completely and then converged on the ceiling, extinguishing the light altogether.

Before Ethan could run, a thin, inky stalactite shot down toward him. He threw himself out of the way just in time. If Blotter got on him, he could cover his face again and suffocate him this time. But Blotter wasn't really interested in Ethan—a second needle shot down, aimed right at Inkling on his hand.

Ethan dodged again and burst out into the hallway. He looked over his shoulder to see a red-tinted shadow boiling along the wall after him like molten lava. Dad barreled toward him, a sloshing bucket in his hand. He hurled the water. It hit Blotter head-on, and instantly the ink sluiced off the wall and pooled in a dirty gray mess.

Ethan felt a cool breeze on his hand and looked down to see Inkling writing:

IT WON'T LAST LONG!

Already the puddle was stirring and getting darker—or rather, the ink was separating itself from the water, pulling free across the floor.

At that moment, Sarah appeared in her bedroom doorway, her sleepy face haloed by tousled hair. Against her chest, she held one of her favorite soft toys, a black dog called Rexy. She looked at the messy puddle on the floor, then up at Dad, and said:

"Oh, Dada, she is very disappointed with you."

"Sarah, go back to bed!" Ethan said. Against her white pajamas, her soft toy looked very black, and very much like an ink splotch.

Blotter must have thought so, too, because with a giant pull, he surged free of the water and went boiling across the floor straight for Sarah.

"No!" Dad shouted, and planted himself in front of her.

"Lucy!" Sarah cried out.

"Over here!" Ethan shouted, waving his arms.

In confusion Blotter swirled on the floor, like a hunting dog who'd momentarily lost the scent. And then he must've found it, because he lurched around to face Ethan.

Ethan ran down the hallway and into the kitchen, Blotter nipping at his heels. He streaked past the poster of King Kong, glimpsed the biplanes, and had an idea.

He bolted into the kitchen and, without slowing, swiped one of Sarah's drawings off the fridge. Into the dining room, the living room, back into the hallway, all the while folding the drawing into a paper airplane.

"Get on!" he whispered to Inkling, making the last sloppy folds. "Hold tight!"

Ethan felt a hot, sweaty grasp around his ankle and knew Blotter was on him now.

"Ethan!" his father shouted, his face creased with worry.

"Get ready!" he said as he ran past.

He felt Blotter's clammy grip climb his leg, then spread out around his waist. It was hard to breathe. When he was nearly at the bathroom, Ethan looked over his shoulder and launched the paper airplane. It sailed back down the hallway to his father, who caught it. Inkling was safe—and Blotter hadn't noticed yet.

Ethan felt Blotter's heat clamping down on his chest, almost at his neck. Ethan burst into the bathroom and suddenly couldn't breathe. Blotter had seeped over his mouth and nose, suffocating him, and then—

He was plunged into total darkness as Blotter covered his eyes.

Desperately he reached out with his hands. Sink. Toilet. He felt Blotter swirling around his head, prodding into his armpits, searching for Inkling.

Ethan was starving for air. His hands found the walk-in shower. He stepped inside and pulled the door shut tight behind him. Wildly he patted the wall for the faucet.

Where are you?

His fingers found it and turned it on full blast. The water was icy cold and he let it wallop him full in the face. He thought he was going to faint. He still couldn't breathe—

Then suddenly he could.

And see! He could see again! He gave a hoarse cheer and looked down. At his soaking feet he saw a grayish swirl.

Blotter was washing off him . . .

And swirling down the drain!

Ethan turned round and round in the shower, making sure the water struck every part of him. The water darkened at his feet as more and more ink ran off him. He could see Blotter sending out tendrils, fighting to climb the walls of the shower. But Ethan aimed the nozzle and blasted Blotter back down. Down the drain he went.

Shivering violently, Ethan made the water warmer. He soaped his skin and clothes all over. Rubbing every inch of himself, until the water at his feet was entirely clear. He kept the water going a bit longer just to make sure, then turned it off. He stood there, panting.

"He's gone!" he shouted.

Dad burst into the bathroom, holding Sarah by the hand. In his other hand was the paper airplane.

"It worked!" Ethan hollered. "He just washed down the drain!"

He stepped out, his clothes heavy and sopping.

"That was quick thinking!" Dad said, throwing a big towel around his shoulders and squeezing him tight. "Amazing!"

They watched the drain. Ethan's heart was still thumping. The last of the water swirled down. A few drips from the faucet hit the tile.

"What have you done with Lucy?" Sarah demanded, scrunching her nose in annoyance.

"He's right here," Dad said, and opened up the paper airplane to reveal Inkling, already in the shape of a puppy, wagging his tail. Dad held the paper to the wall so Inkling could flow off and gambol about near the floor. A speech bubble appeared from his mouth:

SARAH!

"Lucy! You came back!"

WOOF! WOOF!

"Where have you been, you naughty puppy?" Sarah said.

From the shower drain came a mournful faraway whisper. Ethan glanced nervously at Dad. A tortured slurping sound echoed up from the pipes.

"No . . ." Ethan grabbed a rubber plug and jammed it hard into the drain. Through the floorboards came a terrible gurgle, like ten toilets flushing.

Before Ethan could step back, the plug exploded from the drain and hit the ceiling. And then came Blotter. Like an oily geyser, he spewed up, spattering the walls of the shower, then sliding down the tile. In a wave, he crested the lip and poured onto the bathroom floor.

"Ethan, come on!" said Dad, pulling Sarah into his arms and rushing out.

Ethan backed out, but Inkling didn't flee. He slid down onto the floor.

"What're you doing?" Ethan shouted. "Get out!"

Inkling made himself as big as possible and edged toward Blotter, who had pooled outside the shower, greedy tendrils waggling in front of him like those of some enormous bug.

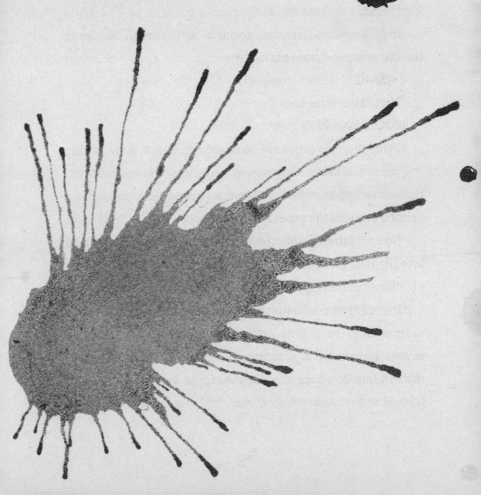

Inkling lunged. Blotter lunged. The two ink splotches slammed into each other. They shoved and twisted and wrestled, and it seemed to Ethan that each was trying to crush the other into himself. But again and again, they pulled away, only to lash out at each other with greater intensity. Blotter was bigger, no question, but Inkling was nimbler. Blotter slugged with huge, inky limbs; Inkling dodged and jabbed.

"Inkling, watch out!" Ethan shouted, because he saw that Blotter was sneakily spreading himself out to either side, trying to outflank him.

Inkling tried to fall back, but too late. Blotter had closed the circle around him. In a split second, the circle thickened and started to fleshily contract.

"No!" cried Ethan.

Blotter swallowed Inkling whole.

Ethan thought he could see Inkling's black body within the red tint of Blotter's. It was like seeing a mouse swallowed by an anaconda and forced down its throat.

Blotter swelled triumphantly. Ethan could almost hear his cry of victory as the reddish ink flexed his muscles and bristled with monster fins and spines.

It's over, Ethan thought in despair.

His dad appeared with another bucket of water and made to throw it.

"Wait!" Ethan told him, because Blotter had just flinched. His inky surface puckered, like a ripple moving out from a thrown stone. Somewhere in the middle he seemed to bulge, as though something under the surface struggled to break free. Ethan pointed.

"It's Inkling!" he shouted as the ripple reached the edge of Blotter and pulled himself out—a solid black splotch.

But Inkling didn't pull free entirely. He stayed connected to Blotter—

And *pulled.*

"He's trying to drag him!" Ethan said.

"Is he strong enough?" Dad asked.

"Look!"

It was like a tiny tug hauling an ocean liner out of the harbor. Blotter fought, trying to break free, sending inky fingers everywhere, digging into the floor, the wall, the doorframe, to slow himself. But nothing slowed him. Jerkily, Inkling kept pulling, heading for—

The studio.

"What's he doing?" Dad asked.

Ethan had no idea. But he could see that Inkling was getting slower, and Blotter was starting to drag him back a little bit now.

"We need to help him!" Ethan said. "Food! He needs pictures and words! The best you can find!"

"Help Lucy!" Sarah cried out from the doorway to her room.

"Yes!" said Dad. "On it!"

He bolted to his studio and raced back, a single book in his hands—a beautifully illustrated collection of stories Ethan remembered from when he was younger. Ethan grabbed it and opened it in front of Inkling. A woman in shining armor. Inkling slid over it, absorbing it and swelling a little. As quickly as he could, Ethan turned the pages. People chanting to end injustice, a dog protecting its owner from a bear, children slaying demons. Inkling ate them all. Bigger and stronger now, he struggled onward, dragging Blotter right into the studio.

"Go, Inkling!" Dad shouted.

"Inkling, drag him into this!" Ethan said, grabbing an empty vase and laying it on the floor.

But Inkling went around the vase.

"What're you doing?" Ethan asked in confusion. If Inkling could drag Blotter into the vase, and get out fast, they might be able to trap Blotter inside.

But Inkling obviously had his own plan.

When he'd hauled Blotter all the way to the drafting table, Ethan began to understand. He felt a huge heaviness on his chest.

"No . . . ," he breathed.

He tried to put his hand in front of Inkling, but Inkling just flowed over him.

"Inkling, stop!" he begged.

Up the leg of the table, Inkling yanked Blotter, but near the top he began to falter. Blotter, with his massive bulk, was dragging him back.

With a bloodcurdling yowl, Rickman lunged at the table

leg and sank his claws into Blotter. Blotter's entire body went watery with panic, and in that moment, Inkling heaved himself and Blotter onto the tabletop.

ETHAN. HELP ME! OPEN THE SKETCHBOOK!

Ethan shook his head.

IT'S THE ONLY WAY!

Peter Rylance stepped forward and, before Ethan could stop him, opened his sketchbook.

The book did the rest.

Neither Inkling nor Blotter could resist its pull. Blotter struggled and farted and belched and spewed ink. He dug in with a thousand inky insect legs, but the gravity of the sketchbook was too great. These thick, creamy pages were Inkling's birthplace, and they wanted every bit of him back.

Blotter, with his greater mass, got pulled in first. Faster and faster, he was dragged onto the paper. The moment the ink touched, it was fixed.

"Inkling, let go!" Ethan shouted, for Inkling was still attached to Blotter.

But he, too, was snapped up onto the pages of the sketchbook.

Everything was suddenly still, like after a thunderstorm has passed.

Beside his father, Ethan stared in amazement at the sketchbook, where two ink splotches, one large and reddish-tinged, the other smaller and intense black, were fixed on the paper, motionless.

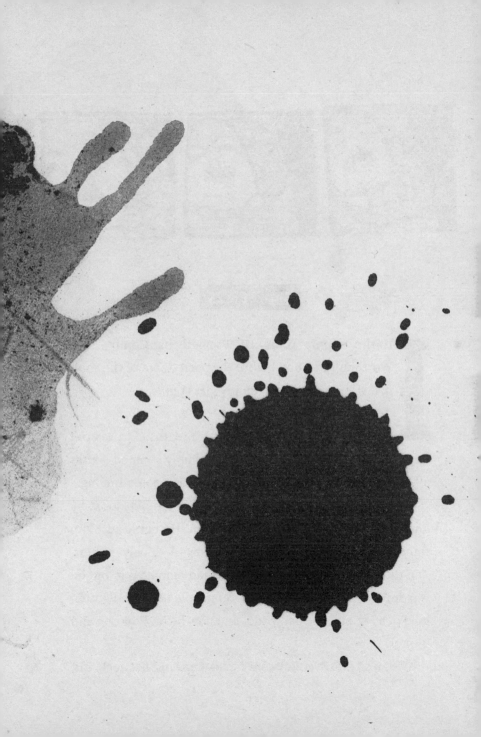

CHAPTER 21

In the supply room of Prometheus Comix, Karl Worthington stood before the open doors of the cabinet, staring at the two empty glass tanks.

Blotter gone. Inkling gone.

He made himself take slow breaths. For a brief moment, he wondered if Blotter had simply escaped—after all, he was getting too big for that tank—and eaten Inkling.

But the ink couldn't have opened the cabinet doors by himself—and wouldn't have needed to. He could just slip right through the cracks. No, this was obviously a theft. Karl didn't know how Peter Rylance had managed it, but he was sure it must have been him. Somehow Peter had gotten hold of a key and the passcode, and now he had Inkling and Blotter.

With a small silver key that he kept around his neck, Mr.

Worthington opened a compartment lower in the cabinet. He allowed himself a small smile.

After he'd moved Blotter into the office, he'd chopped off a few little bits of him with the big paper cutter. A couple quick, hard swings of the blade. Just as an experiment, just to be sure.

"Hey, little guys," he said, reaching into the compartment.

One by one he lifted out three glass jars. In each was a swirling red-tinged ink splotch.

"You guys are going to do great things," Mr. Worthington said.

CHAPTER 22

"Lucy!" said Sarah sternly. "You are a very naughty puppy!"

The Labradoodle puppy ignored her and continued chewing one of Sarah's favorite soft toys on the living room floor.

"You wicked dog," said Sarah with huge enjoyment. She dropped her face close to the puppy's and giggled as Lucy licked her enthusiastically.

"That tickles," said Sarah with delight.

Ethan couldn't imagine a happier face.

"I never wanted a dog," Dad said, "but this makes it almost worth it."

"She's pretty cute," Ethan said.

"She's very cute," Dad said. "I'm probably going to spoil the thing rotten."

Rickman cautiously entered the room and looked balefully at Lucy. When the puppy saw the cat, she scrambled to her feet and growled and yipped. Rickman bristled and started to slink away.

"Lucy, no!" said Sarah, tapping the puppy gently on the head. "Icklan is nice."

And she went over to Rickman and gave him a quick stroke. Rickman stood there, stunned, then sank down on the floor, purring contentedly.

"I *like* Icklan," Sarah said.

Ethan looked over at his dad. "Do you believe it?"

"Yeah, finally, she likes the cat."

"Yeah, but did you notice she used the word *I*? 'I like Icklan'!"

"You're right!" Dad said, grinning. "Good talking, Sarah!"

"She knows," Sarah said, and went back to Lucy.

While Dad and Sarah played with the new puppy, Ethan went to his bedroom. It had been two weeks since he'd rescued Inkling—and then lost him to the sketchbook.

Lost. That was absolutely how Ethan thought of it. He'd truly lost a friend, and he missed him.

On his top shelf, where Ethan kept all his favorite things, was the sketchbook. Even though there were still plenty of blank pages left, Dad had retired it as a memorial to Inkling.

Sitting down on his bed, Ethan opened it up and found the pages where Blotter and Inkling were fixed. He touched Inkling, but no breezy sensation moved against his fingertips. There was no life or energy, just dry ink. A few days ago, he thought he'd seen a flicker of movement, but it was just his eyes playing tricks on him.

Inkling was truly gone.

. . .

"I was very impressed with the quality of your graphic novels," said Ms. D as she handed them back to the groups. "And I was especially pleased with how well you all collaborated and divided up the work."

Ethan crowded around his project with Soren, Pino, and Brady. Pino had done a fantastic job with the coloring, and Ethan was impressed by how much energy and personality it had added to the graphic novel. And Brady had surprised everyone with how neat his lettering was, and how he'd experimented with different styles and colors, depending on who was talking and what was happening in the scene.

On the very last page, Ms. D had paper-clipped her comments.

"'A highly imaginative and original story,'" Ethan read, nudging Soren. "That's you!"

"'Exquisite coloring,'" said Pino with a grin.

"'The lettering was done with great care and panache,'" said Brady. "What's *panache*?"

"It means you didn't use too much correction fluid," said Pino.

"Yeah, I was really careful," Brady said. "What's she say about the artwork?"

Ethan read aloud. "'While the artwork was of a generally high standard, greater care could have been taken with smudges.'" Ethan grinned, remembering how he'd asked Inkling to mess up the art on purpose. "'The last third of the project seemed a bit rushed as the artwork was not as strong, and quite a bit messier.'"

"I don't know what she's talking about," Soren said to him.

"Guys, who cares?" said Brady, pointing at their letter grade. "We got an A!"

Pino went on a recon mission to check out everyone else's grades. Ethan paged through the spreads. He couldn't help feeling wistful as he looked at all the images Inkling had drawn—especially toward the end, when Inkling had been teaching him how to draw. He'd never forget how much fun it was, working together.

"I think you should keep it," Soren said to him.

"No, we'll split it up," Ethan said. "We all did this. Everyone should take their favorite spreads. I wouldn't mind having the last few pages."

"Great mark," said Heather Lee, leaning over to have a look. "Congratulations."

"Thanks," said Ethan, blushing. "How'd you guys do?"

"B-plus," she said, and shrugged. "Not all of us can draw like you."

"I'm not that good," Ethan said. "I had *a lot* of help."

Pino came back to their table and said indignantly, "Vika's group got an A-*plus*."

"What?" Brady said. "Ours was way better!"

"No fair!" said Pino.

"It's fair," Ethan said. He'd seen Vika's work when she'd handed it in. "Believe me, it is *totally* fair."

He looked across the room at Vika, who was talking with her group. When she glanced over at him, he mouthed, "Congratulations."

She nodded, and almost smiled.

• • •

"Hey, I wanted to show you something," Dad said when Ethan got home from school. "I started something new today."

"That's great!" Ethan said, then frowned. "So you're not going to finish the one you started with Inkling?"

Dad shook his head. "There was something missing."

"What do you mean?"

"The artwork was wonderful; the story was solid. But there wasn't one thing original about it."

Ethan felt offended on Inkling's behalf. "He'd been working so hard on it!"

"I know. And you taught him well, giving him all my books, and good stuff other people have done. But that's what it felt like. A kind of mishmash of really great stuff that's already been done. I need to do something truly new. On my own."

"Okay." Ethan could understand that.

"You know," Dad said to him as they walked down the hall, "I was thinking about your drawing."

"I'll never be very good," Ethan said. Even though Inkling had helped him improve, he knew he'd never be as talented as his dad, and it made him discouraged.

"Not true," Dad said. "First of all, you've got a lot of years ahead of you to learn. But also, those stick figures you do?"

"What about them?"

"They're really good."

Ethan turned to his dad in amazement. "They're just stupid stick figures. They're, like, nothing."

Dad shook his head. "No. They have a ton of personality. And energy. The positions you draw them in, they're really expressive."

Ethan felt his cheeks heat up. "Honest?"

"And even better, no one else does anything like it. It could be your thing."

"Huh," said Ethan. He still wasn't sure drawing was his thing, period, but maybe Dad was right and it was too early to say. "Thanks."

"So let me show you my new stuff," Dad said inside the studio.

"Are you doing another Kren?"

Dad laughed. "No. I thought it was time to do something a little more personal. Something under our own roof."

Ethan leaned against the drafting table and looked at the double-page spread.

The first panels were wordless.

There was a house, which looked a lot like theirs, at night, the windows dark.

There was the hallway, deserted and quiet.

A cat prowled along. He was a handsomer version of Rickman, eating something from the carpet.

There was a studio. A small flex lamp had been left on, illuminating the drafting table and the gleaming pages of an open sketchbook.

Closer.

The cat leapt up onto the chair and put his paws on the edge of the table.

Closer still.

The ink in the sketchbook glistened, then moved.

And then, finally, a caption:

No one was awake to see it happen, except Rickman.

THE INVASION HAS BEGUN.

THE OVERTHROW BOOK 1

BLOOM

KENNETH OPPEL

Turn the page for a glimpse of
Kenneth Oppel's infectious new series.

Using the chopsticks, Mr. Riggs delicately gripped the plant and eased it out through the neck. Seeing it spread flat on the cutting board, Petra was surprised how big the leaves were. All this, just overnight, in the darkness of the medicine cabinet. She looked at their fine black veins, the tiny hairs.

"The leaves are quite fleshy," Mr. Riggs said, handling them gently. "Perfectly symmetrical. And see." He touched a small bulge in the plant's center. "I think this might be a flowering stem beginning here. It reminds me of a water lily."

"Same black color as the grass," Petra said. "You think they're related, Mr. Riggs?"

"Possibly. Let's have a look at this last one."

At the sink, he poured out the third bottle and returned with the colander. Resting on the bottom were the three black peas. Petra frowned. The tiny shoots looked longer than they had inside the bottle.

"These guys," Mr. Riggs remarked, "look a bit like very tiny bulbs."

"Does that mean they're flowers?" Petra asked.

"Could be. A flower bulb usually has multiple roots at the bottom, though. These guys just have a single shoot growing from this bud here, right at the pointy end." He picked up one of the bulbs. "They're very young. The shoots are still undifferentiated."

"Undifferentiated?" she asked, and was sorry she did, because Anaya answered.

"They haven't started forming leaves or branching off yet."

Petra caught Mr. Riggs give his daughter an approving nod, and tried not to roll her eyes.

Her own dad asked, "Have you seen anything like this, Mike?"

"No. And it's hard to know what this one's going to become."

As he held it close to his face, Petra saw a bead of fluid leak from the bulb onto the pad of his thumb.

"Huh," Mr. Riggs said, setting down the bulb and sniffing the liquid. He rubbed it between his fingertips, then frowned. Abruptly he stood up and hurried to the sink.

"Dad?" Anaya said worriedly.

Mr. Riggs turned on the tap and held his hand under the water.

"That has a nasty sting to it," he said over his shoulder. "Don't touch it."

"Let's take a look," Petra's dad said.

When Mr. Riggs turned, Petra could see the angry blisters on his fingertips.

"Hard to tell if it's an allergic reaction, or an acid burn," her dad said.

She looked back down at the bulb, and gave a cry as its shoot twitched.

"Holy crap! It just moved!"

"I saw it, too!" Anaya said.

Their eyes met, and for just a second it was like they were friends again.

"You sure, Petra?" her dad asked.

"Yeah! It was like it just . . . grew. Does it look a little longer to you guys?"

She didn't know much about plants, but you weren't supposed to be able to *see* them growing.

"Anaya," Mr. Riggs said, "could you get some Ziploc bags and wet paper towel to pack these things up? Put on gloves before handling the bulbs."

"Sure thing."

"Thanks for bringing these, Petra," Mr. Riggs said. "This is incredibly useful." He pointed at the bulbs and the bat-leafed plant. "I haven't seen reports of these varieties yet." He shook his head. "Three new plant species in one sample of rainwater—seems like quite a coincidence, doesn't it?"

"So, you think it's possible?" she asked him. "The seeds were actually in the rain?"

"Hard to dismiss," Mr. Riggs said.

Petra cut a sidelong glance at Anaya. She couldn't help gloating. Maybe she was the first person to come up with the idea—the first person who wasn't crazy, anyway.

"So, hang on," said her father. "If the seeds were all delivered together, it means someone's doing this, right? Bioterrorism?"

Mr. Riggs nodded gravely. "I'll be calling the Ministry."

Petra watched Anaya packing the plants into Ziploc bags. "Is it safe for me to keep washing with the water? Because of the seeds, I mean."

Mr. Riggs considered her question. "Well, it hasn't hurt you so far. But probably best not to." He held up his red fingertips. "You don't want anything like this getting on your skin or eyes."

"Okay." She nodded, trying to hide her disappointment. "So, what happens next?"

"I'll transplant these seedlings at the farm," Mr. Riggs said, "and grow them in controlled conditions. We need to know what else we're facing."